选一种姿态 让自己活得无可替代

[英]杰克·奥尔索普 等著

张白桦 译

世界微型小说精选

智慧卷（中英双语）

中国国际广播出版社

图书在版编目（CIP）数据

选一种姿态　让自己活得无可替代：英汉对照 /（英）杰克·奥尔索普等著；张白桦译. —北京：中国国际广播出版社，2019.9
（译趣坊. 世界微型小说精选）
ISBN 978-7-5078-4522-8

Ⅰ.①选… Ⅱ.①杰…②张… Ⅲ.①小小说－小说集－英国－现代－汉、英 Ⅳ.①I561.45

中国版本图书馆CIP数据核字（2019）第192195号

选一种姿态　让自己活得无可替代（中英双语）

著　　者	[英] 杰克·奥尔索普 等
译　　者	张白桦
策　　划	张娟平
责任编辑	高　婧　张娟平
版式设计	国广设计室
责任校对	张　娜

出版发行	中国国际广播出版社 [010-83139469　010-83139489（传真）]
社　　址	北京市西城区天宁寺前街2号北院A座一层
	邮编：100055
网　　址	www.chirp.com.cn
经　　销	新华书店
印　　刷	环球东方（北京）印务有限公司

开　　本	880×1230　1/32
字　　数	200千字
印　　张	7.25
版　　次	2019年10月　北京第一版
印　　次	2019年10月　第一次印刷
定　　价	28.00元

CRI　欢迎关注本社新浪官方微博　版权所有
中国国际广播出版社　官方网站 www.chirp.cn　盗版必究

·代○序·

微型小说界的一个奇异存在

陈春水

张白桦，女，于1963年4月出生于辽宁沈阳一个世代书香的知识分子家庭，父亲是中国第一代俄语专业大学生。她曾先后就读于三所高校，具有双专业教育背景，所修专业分别为英国语言文学、比较文学与世界文学。两次跳级经历，一次是从初二到高三，一次是从大一到大二。最后学历为上海外国语大学文学硕士，研究方向为译介学，师从谢天振教授（国际知名比较文学专家与翻译理论家、译介学创始人、中国翻译学创建人、比较文学终身奖获得者），为英美文学研究专家、翻译家胡允桓（与杨宪益、沙博理、赵萝蕤、李文俊、董乐山同获"中美文学交流奖"，诺贝尔文学奖得主托妮·莫里森世界范围内研究兼汉译第一人，翻译终身奖获得者）私淑弟子。她现为内蒙古工业大学外国语学院副教授、硕士研究生导师，并兼任中国比较文学学会翻译研究会理事、上海翻译家协会会员、内蒙古作家协会会员。张白桦于1987年开始文学创作，已在《读者》《中外期刊文萃》《青年博览》《小小说选刊》《青年参考》《文学故事报》等海内外一百多种报刊，以及生活·读书·新知三联书店、中译出版社、北京大学出版社、中国国际广播出版社，公开出版以微型小说翻译为主，包括长篇小说、中篇小说、散文、随笔、诗歌、杂文、评论翻译和原创等在内的编著译作30部，累计1200万字。

在中国微型小说界，众所周知的是：以性别而论，男性译作者多，女性译作者少；以工作内容而论，搞创作的多，搞研究的少；以文学样式而论，只创作微型小说的作者多，同时创作长篇小说、散文、诗歌、文学评论的作者少；以作者性质而论，搞原创的多，搞翻译的少；以翻译途径而论，外译汉的译者多，汉译外的译者少；以译者而论，搞翻译的人多，同时搞原创的人少。而具备上述所有"少"于一身的奇异存在，恐怕张白桦是绝无仅有的一位。

张白桦是当代中国微型小说第一代译作者，也是唯一因微型小说翻译而获奖的翻译家。译作量大质优，覆盖面广泛，风格鲜明，具有女性文学史、微型小说史意义；是中国第一个从理论上，从宏观和微观层面，论证当代外国微型小说汉译的文学史意义的学者，具有翻译文学史意义；小说创作篇幅涉及长篇、中篇、短篇、微型小说，创作的文学样式覆盖小说、散文、诗歌、文学评论等主要文学样式；是既有微型小说译作，又有微型小说原创的全能型译作家，且译作与原创具有通约性；还是微型小说英汉双向翻译的译作者。

她的微型小说翻译实践开创了中国微型小说双向翻译的两个第一："译趣坊"系列图书为中国首部微型小说译文集，在美国出版的《凌鼎年微型小说选集》为中国首部微型小说自选集英译本。

2002年微型小说译著《英汉经典阅读系列散文卷》曾获上海外国语大学研究生学术文化节科研成果奖；1998年微型小说译作《爱旅无涯》获《中国青年报·青年参考》最受读者喜爱的翻译文学作品；她本人曾在2001年当选小小说存档作家、2002年当选为当代微型小说百家；微型小说译作《仇家》当选为全国第四次微型小说续写大赛竞赛原作；2012年译作《海妖的诱惑》获以色列第32届世界诗人大会主席奖等文学奖项；"译趣坊"系列图书深受广大青年读者喜欢。

此外，她的论文《外国微型小说在中国的初期接受》入选复旦大学出版社的《润物有声——谢天振教授七十华诞纪念文集》，以及湖南大学出版社的张春的专著《中国小小说六十年》续表。译作《门把手》入选春风文艺出版社出版的《21世纪中国文学大系2002年翻译文学》。译作《生命倒计时》入选春风文艺出版社出版的谢天振、韩忠良的专著《21世纪中国文学大系2010年翻译文学》。

张白桦关于外国微型小说的论文具有前沿性和开拓意义。例如，《外国微型小说在中国的初期接受》是国内对于外国微型小说在中国接受的宏观梳理和微观分析。《当代外国微型小说汉译的文学史意义》证实了"微型小说翻译与微型小说原创具有同样建构民族、国别文学发展史的意义,即翻译文学应该,也只能是中国文学的一部分"。她指出,当代外国微型小说汉译的翻译文学意义在于:"推动中国当代的主流文学重归文学性,重归传统诗学的'文以载道'的传统;引进并推动确立了一种新型的、活力四射的文学样式;当代微型小说汉译提高了文学的地位,直接催生并参与改写了中国当代文学史,以一种全新的文体重塑了当代主流诗学。"

其论文也反映出张白桦的文学翻译观和文学追求,例如,在《外国微型小说在中国的初期接受》中,她说:"吾以吾手译吾心。以文化和文学的传播为翻译的目的,以妇女儿童和青年为目标读者,让国人了解世界上其他民族的妇女儿童和青年的生存状态。以'归化'为主,'异化'为辅的翻译策略,全译为主,节译和编译为辅,突出译作的影响作用和感化作用,从而形成了简洁隽永、抒情、幽默、时尚的翻译风格。与此同时,译作与母语原创的微型小说,在思想倾向、语言要素、风格类型和审美趣味上形成了通约性和文化张力,丰富了译作的艺术表现力和感染力。"

在《当代外国微型小说汉译的文学史意义》中,她说:"文学翻译是创造性叛逆,创造性叛逆赋予原作以第二次生命,处于文学样式'真空状态'的中国第一代微型小说译者一方面充分发挥了翻译的主体性作用,挥洒着'创造性叛逆'所带来的'豪杰'范儿,对于原文和原语文化'傲娇'地'引进并抵抗着',有意和无意地遵循着自己的文学理想和审美趣味'舞蹈'着,为翻译文学披上了'中国红'的外衣，在内容和形式上赋予译作一种崭新的面貌和第二次生命。一方面在原文、意识形态、经济利益、诗学观念的'镣铐'上，'忠实'并'妥协'着。"

著名评论家张锦贻在《亭亭白桦秀译林》中说："张白桦所译的作品范围极广，涉及世界各大洲，但选择的标准却极严，注重原作表现生活的力度和反映社会的深度。显然，张白桦对于所译原作的这种选择，绝不仅仅是出于爱好，而是反映出她的审美意识和情感倾向。她着力在译作中揭示不同地区、不同国度、不同社会、不同人种的生存境况和心理状态，揭示东西方之间的文化差异和分歧，都显示出她是从人性和人道的角度来观察现实的人生。而正是通过这样的观察，才使她能够真正地去接触各国文学中那些反映社会底层的大众作品，才能使她真正地关注儿童和青年，也才使她的译作真正地走向中国的民众。事实证明，译作的高品位必伴以译者识见的高明和高超。脱了思想内核，怕是做不好文学译介工作的。……类似的译作比比皆是，到后来，就是事先不知道译者，几行读下来，亦能将她给'认出来'。也就是说，张白桦在选择原作和自己的翻译文字上都在逐步形成一种独具的风格。……使她能够在不同的译作中巧用俚语，活用掌故，借用时俗。她善于用中国人最能领会的词语来表达各式各样的口吻，由此活现出不同人物的身份和此时此刻的心神和表情；她也长于用青少年最能领悟的词句来表达不同的侧面，同时展现出不同社会的氛围和当时当地的风习。"

胡晓在《中国教育报》发表的《学英语您捕捉到快乐了吗》："我最喜欢她的译作,因为所选篇目均为凝练精巧之作,难易适中,且多是与生活息息相关的内容,能够极大限度地接近读者。所选的文字皆为沙里淘金的名家经典,文华高远,辞采华丽。名家的经典带来的是审美的享受和精神的愉悦,含蓄隽永的语句令人不由得会心一笑;至真至纯的爱与情,轻轻拨动着人们的神经;睿智透彻的思考,让人旷达而超脱。"

综上所述,在微型小说的文化地理中,张白桦是一个独特的所在。她以独特的文化品相,承接了中华与西洋的博弈,以理论和实践造就的衍生地带,自绘版图却无人能袭。

(作者系中国作协会员,小小说作家网特约评论家,第六届小小说金麻雀提名奖获得者,本篇原载于中国作家网2015年9月9日 http://www.chinawriter.com.cn)

没有微型小说汉译就没有当代微型小说

——张白桦访谈录

陈勇（中国作协会员，小小说作家网特约评论家，第六届小小说金麻雀提名奖获得者，以下简称陈）：我做微型小说评论多年，范围遍及世界华文微型小说界，您是我研究视野中出现的第一个微型小说翻译家，可能也是唯一的一个。

张白桦（以下简称张）：谢谢陈老师的青睐，我更加惊诧于您的学术识别力。因为，即使在外语界和翻译界，对于文学翻译的认识还是有许多误区的。难怪微型小说界的评论总是视译者为"局外人"，所以无人问津了。而从我的研究方向——译介学的角度来看，得出的结论是：微型小说翻译，特别是微型小说翻译文学，应该，也只是中国文学的一部分。

陈：我认同翻译与创作是国别文学的"鸟之两翼，车之两轮"之说，您能给大家普及一下文学翻译与文学创作的区别吗？

张：好的，我愿意。从文艺的本质规律来看，二者并没有分别。

从创作的内容来看，翻译的确比创作少了一道工序——构思。然而，也正是由于这一缺失，反而给翻译带来了创作所没有的困难。可以负责任地说，从创作的过程来看，正如许许多多20世纪三四十年代的作家兼翻译家共同体会到的那样，文学翻译比文学创作要难。

陈：我之所以选择了您作为评论对象，是由于您在微型小说界的独特地位和影响力，以及您在研究和实践层面的全面开花的成果。

张：这倒是符合事实的。在实践方面，我在20世纪80年代初，也就是大三的时候，就翻译了第一篇微型小说，一直走下来，应该说与当代中国微型小说是共同成长的，又是唯一一个因此获奖的译者；此外，中国首部微型小说译文集"译趣坊"系列图书和中国首部微型小说自选集英译本《凌鼎年微型小说选集》也是我做的。在研究方面，是中国第一个从理论上，从宏观和微观层面，论证当代外国微型小说汉译的文学史意义的学人。

陈：您能把您的理论观点论述得详细些吗？

张：可以，当代外国微型小说汉译的翻译文学意义就在于：推动中国当代的主流文学重归文学性，重归传统诗学的"文以载道"的传统；引进并推动确立了一种新型的、活力四射的文学样式；当代微型小说汉译提高了文学的地位，直接催生并参与改写了中国当代文学史，以一种全新的文体重塑了当代主流诗学。

陈：哦，所以您才会下这样的判断："没有外国微型小说汉译，就没有当代微型小说。"是吗？

张：您的学术敏感度令人惊叹。

陈：根据我的调查统计分析，发现搞微型小说翻译实践的人虽然相对不多，却也还是有一些的，您能谈谈使您脱颖而出的"别裁之处"吗？

张：我是经历了实践—理论—再实践这样一个非线性的过程，它带给我的是对文学翻译本质的思考，对翻译艺术掌控力的把握，对文学翻译的全面观照。据我所知，微型小说译者的文化背景比较复杂，创作态度也良莠不齐，老一辈翻译家在语言文化基础和创作态度上是无可厚非的，基本表现为"全译"，可惜在文字上与原文"靠得太近"，人数也太少；中青年译者的数量居多，但语言文化基础大多不如前辈，在对原文的处理上"尺度过大"，多数表现为"编译"。

我生性保守，为人为文拘谨，记得曾经在《世界华文微型小说作家微自传》中这样总结过，"回首往事，也算是'张三中'吧：'心中'的原文，'眼中'的译文，'意中'的师生"。换句话说，对原文的敬畏，对译文的时代化，对青年、妇女儿童读者的念念不忘，千方百计地贴近时代，可能因此造就我的译文忠实性和可读性较强，基本表现为"全译"。

陈：果然如此，在您的译作中，我发现有几个题材是您情有独钟的，比如，青年、妇女和儿童，也就是说这是您自觉的文学追求，是您的"主观倾向"吧？

张：您一语中的。是的，身为女性，我"含泪的微笑"更多地落在了相似群体身上，是希望通过译作擦亮人文关怀的"镜与灯"。

陈：如果让您用几个关键词来概括您的翻译风格的话，您会选择哪些词？

张：首先进入我脑海的是：简洁、幽默、时尚。

陈：为什么是这三个词，而不是其他？

张：这个嘛，都缘于我的"本色演出"，我人简单直接，译文也就长不了；身为教书匠，我喜欢寓教于乐，译文也就搞文字狂欢；我的目标读者是青年，我的译文就各种"潮"，"一大波流行词语正在靠近"。

陈：嗯嗯，听出来啦。

最后，我还是要不客气地指出您在创作趋势上的一个问题，您的微型小说翻译在初期量大质优，"凡有井水处，皆能歌柳词"。而在近期却在数量上大不如前了，希望您可以有所弥补。

张：谢谢陈老师指教，我也意识到了这个问题。原因是多方面的，最重要的还是我目前的长篇著译、教学和研究生辅导让我分身乏术，不过，我一定竭尽心力，在理论上继续为微型小说翻译"鼓与呼"，在实践上做"颜色不一样的烟火"。

（本篇原载于中国作家网 2015 年 9 月 9 日 http://www.chinawriter.com.cn）

目 录
content

我和碧小姐 / Me & Miss Bee · 1

光盘 / A Clean Plate · 8

丑女 / The Ugly Girl · 20

勒赎信 / Ransom Note · 29

"贫穷是什么？" / "What Is Poverty?" · 36

圆满的结局 / Happy Endings · 49

入职介绍 / Orientation · 60

2053 年的夜行人 / The Pedestrian · 77

身体最重要的部位 / What Is the Most Important Part of the Body · 85

诚实的乞丐 / An Honest Beggar · 89

机智的女儿 / Thinking Out of the Box · 96

红蚂蚁大战黑蚂蚁 / The Battle of the Red and the Black Ants · 100

夏夜 / One Summer Night · 105

骆驼为什么有驼峰 / How the Camel Got His Hump · 110

房子上的藤蔓 / A Vine on a House · 119

最好的朋友 / Best Friends · 128

石狮子 / The Stone Lion · 134

为什么海水是咸的 / The Magic Mill · 141

雪人 / The Snowman · 151

有症状的乘客 / The Sympathetic Passenger · 160

化敌为友 / Worst Enemy-Best Friends · 171

不要告诉我我很漂亮 / Don't Tell Me I'm Beautiful · 185

应急预案 / Contingency Plan · 192

活着 / Love of Life · 201

死如树脂 / Sap · 208

我和碧小姐

[美国] 杰基·克莱门茨－马伦达

你去肉铺买肉,去药房买阿司匹林,去食品杂货店买食品,这都很容易。可那年夏天我待在纽约州沃里克镇奶奶家时,情况则不一样。她写了一张购物清单叫我到一家综合商店买东西。杂货店货架上的商品满满当当地胡乱堆在一起,我怎么才能找到要买的东西啊?

我走近柜台,柜台后面有一位我从来没有见过的女士。一副镶有假宝石边框的眼镜摇摇欲坠地架在她的鼻尖上,头上一堆灰白色的头发。

"打扰一下。"我说。女人抬起了头。

"你就是克莱门特家的小孩吧。"她说,"我是碧小姐。过来让我好好看看。"碧小姐把眼镜向鼻子上扶了扶说道,"如果商店丢了什么东西的话,我好向治安官描述你的外貌特征。"

"我又不是小偷!"我大吃一惊。我才七岁啊,这么小怎么可能当小偷呢!

"在我看来,你只是个黄毛丫头,可我觉得你有这方面的潜质。"碧小姐说着就回过头看报纸去了。

"我要买这些东西。"我说着,举起手里的购物单给她看。

"那又怎样？自己去拿呀。" 碧小姐用手指了一下纱门上的一块牌子。"这里除了你我再没别人，我不是你的仆人，所以我建议你最好从那边那堆篮子里拿一个，找到要买的东西就往里面放。如果幸运的话，你可以在日头落下去之前赶到家。"

离天黑还有五个小时，我不知道来不来得及。

我从离我最近的货架开始寻找购物单上第一件商品：猪肉和菜豆。我从这面墙到那面墙来来回回找了三次，才在一堆面包和麦片里发现一听猪肉。第二件是一卷卫生纸，是在一份日报下找到的；创可贴——我在哪儿看到的？哦，对了，在面霜旁边。这家商店就像一座迷宫，然而里面却充满惊喜。我还在花生酱后面发现塞着一本新的超人漫画。

那年夏天，我每个星期都要去几次碧小姐的综合店铺。有时候，碧小姐会少找给我钱；有时候，她会多收我钱；要不就把前一天的旧报纸当作当天的报纸卖给我。我到她店里买东西，感觉就像一场战斗。我离开奶奶家，手里攥着购物单，心中牢记商品名的拼写，向碧小姐的综合商店前进，简直就像当年征战北非的巴顿将军。

"那听菜豆只有二十九美分！"一天下午，我纠正碧小姐道。我紧盯着收款机上的数字变化，碧小姐入账时记的是三十五美分。被我察觉多收了钱后，碧小姐一点儿尴尬的样子都没有，她越过镜框瞥了我一眼，然后把价格改了过来。

她从不让我宣告胜利。整个夏天，她想尽办法来捉弄我。我刚记住小苏打的发音以及它在货架上的位置，她就调整了商品的排列，害得我重新定位。夏天快结束了，以前要耗费我一小时的购物之旅，现在十五分钟就完事了。在我要返回布鲁克林的那天早上，我到碧小姐综合店买一包口香糖。

"好了，潜能小姐，"她说，"这个夏天你都学到了什么？"你是一个吝啬鬼！我双唇紧闭，没有把心里的话说出来。令人惊奇的是，碧小姐哈哈大笑起来。"我知道你是怎么看我的。"她说。"嗯，你不会想到，我并不在意！我们每个人都被放在这个地球上是有原因的。我相信我的任务就是教会我遇到的每个孩子人生的十个道理。随便你怎么想，潜能小姐。当你再长大一些以后，就会意识到我们的路有交集其实是一件让人高兴的事。"很高兴认识碧小姐？哈！这想法够荒谬的……

直到有一天，女儿带着作业上的问题来找我。

"这些数学题太难做了，你能帮我做吗？"她说。

"如果妈妈帮你做了，那你怎么能学会自己做呢？"我反问道。就在那一瞬间，我突然想起那时在碧小姐的综合商店的情景：我吃力地清点我的账单，核对着收款机里的数字。自那时起，我有被多收过钱吗？

当我的女儿回过头继续做作业时，我琢磨着：多年前，碧小姐真的教授了我若干人生道理吗？我随手拿起了纸，开始把它们写出来。

确实，我学到了整整十条人生道理：

1. 学会仔细倾听。
2. 不要想当然——今非昔比，每天都有新变化。
3. 生活处处有惊喜。
4. 畅所欲言，提出你的问题。
5. 摆脱困境只能靠自己。
6. 并不是每一个人都像你一样诚实。
7. 不要急于评判他人。
8. 凡事要竭尽全力，就算并非能力所及。
9. 反复检查所完成的一切。
10. 良师处处有，不仅限于学校。

Me & Miss Bee

By Jackie Clements-Marenda

You went to the butcher's for meat, the pharmacy for aspirin, and the grocery store for food. But when I spent the summer with my grandmother in Warwick, N.Y., she sent me down to the general store with a list. How could I hope to find anything on the packed, jumbled shelves around me?

I walked up to the counter. Behind it was a lady like no one I'd ever seen. Fake-jewel-encrusted glasses teetered on the tip of her nose, gray hair was piled on her head.

"Excuse me," I said. She looked up.

"You're that Clements kid," she said. "I'm Miss Bee. Come closer and let me get a look at you." She pushed her glasses up her nose. "I want to be able to describe you to the sheriff if something goes missing from the store."

"I'm not a thief!" I was shocked. I was seven year too young to be a thief!

"From what I can see you're not much of anything. But

I can tell you've got potential." She went back to reading her newspaper.

"I need to get these." I said, holding up my list.

"So? Go get them." Miss Bee pointed to a sign on the screen door. "There's no one here except you and me and I'm not your servant, so I suggest you get yourself a basket from that pile over there and start filling. If you're lucky you'll be home by sundown."

Sundown was five hours away. I wasn't sure I would make it.

I scanned the nearest shelf for the first item on my list: pork and beans. It took me three wall-to-wall searches before I found a can nestled between boxes of cereal and bread. Next up was toilet paper, found under the daily newspaper. Band-Aids — where had I seen them? Oh, ye next to the face cream. The store was a puzzle, but it held some surprises, too. I found a new Superman comic tucked behind the peanut butter.

I visited Miss Bee a couple of times a week that summer. Sometimes she short-changed me. Other times she overcharged. Or sold me an old newspaper instead of one that was current. Going to the store was more like going into battle. I left my Grandma's house armed with my list — memorized to the letter — and marched into Miss Bee's like General Patton marching into North Africa.

"That can of beans is only twenty-nine cents!" I corrected her one afternoon. I had watched the numbers change on the cash register closely, and Miss Bee had added 35 cents. She didn't seem embarrassed that I had caught her overcharging. She just looked at me over her glasses and fixed the price.

Not that she ever let me declare victory. All summer long she found ways to trip me up. No sooner had I learned how to pronounce bicarbonate of soda and memorized its location on the shelf, than Miss Bee rearranged the shelves and made me hunt for it all over again. By summer's end the shopping trip that had once taken me an hour was done in 15 minutes. The morning I was to return to Brooklyn, I stopped in to get a packet of gum.

"All right, Miss Potential," she said. "What did you learn this summer?" That you're a meany! I pressed my lips together. To my amazement, Miss Bee laughed. "I know what you think of me," she said. "Well, here's a news flash: I don't care! Each of us is put on this earth for a reason. I believe my job is to teach every child I meet ten life lessons to help them. Think what you will, Miss Potential, but when you get older you'll be glad our paths crossed!" Glad I met Miss Bee? Ha! The idea was absurd…

Until one day my daughter came to me with homework troubles.

"It's too hard," she said. "Could you finish my math problems for me?"

"If I do it for you how will you ever learn to do it yourself?" I said. Suddenly, I was back at that general store where I had learned the hard way to tally up my bill along with the cashier. Had I ever been overcharged since?

As my daughter went back to her homework, I wondered: Had Miss Bee really taught me something all those years ago? I took out some scrap paper and started writing.

Sure enough, I had learned ten life lessons:

1. Listen well.

2. Never assume—things aren't always the same as they were yesterday.

3. Life is full of surprises.

4. Speak up and ask questions.

5. Don't expect to be bailed out of a predicament.

6. Everyone isn't as honest as I try to be.

7. Don't be so quick to judge other people.

8. Try my best, even when the task seems beyond me.

9. Double-check everything.

10. The best teachers aren't only in school.

光 盘

　　1879年，加利福尼亚东南部的一个小镇在三位数的温度下烘烤着。此时下午将近，从中午开始，外面就几乎看不见人了。这时，一个人骑着马出现了，从正东而来。主街只是条小径的延伸，他跑过整条主街抵达小径以后，黑色的眼睛左顾右盼，把一切尽收眼底。他在小镇最西头的一个有仆人的马厩前停了下来，把马匹留在那里，自己回头向东走去，在中国人乔的小饭馆前停下了脚步。

　　这位陌生人站在路边，掸了掸衣服上的土，他头上戴的尖帽子、上身穿的衬衫以及脚上穿的靴子都是黑色的，外面套的短夹克和下身穿的裤子是海军蓝色，几个地方已经磨得发亮。唯一与他通身的深色装扮形成鲜明对照的是两把45式柯尔特左轮手枪的白色骨柄。这种枪以"和平缔造者"而闻名，可是，这个称号却不适合这个持枪的人。他进了小饭馆，猛地用力把门推开，门从金属挡板上猛地弹回来，然后向后摔去，砰的一声关上了，小木屋随之一震。

　　中国人乔在这个镇子上住了六年，已经成了当地的名人。没有人知道他的真名，除了他自己，也没有人记得他这个绰号的由来。尽管他的英语说得还过得去，可是他少言寡语，从来没有泄露过他的背景。他到小镇一个星期不到，就摆开桌子供应美味佳肴了，既有中国菜，也有美国菜。他的饭菜那么好吃，所以附近旅馆的服务员宁可不吃旅馆免费的饭菜，也要自己花钱吃他做的饭菜。除了美食的诱惑外，人们去他的饭馆还因为他的颜值：他身高6英尺5英寸，身材瘦削，总是穿着一件精致的丝绸长袍，上面的图案醒目，有红、黄、黑、绿四种颜色。不论他在厨房待多长时间，这件华美的服饰看起来总是干净利落。

在中国人乔的饭馆里，气氛是安静而舒缓的，仿佛他用自己安静的个性浸透了这幢房子。唯一的一次骚乱发生在他来这里的数月之后，一个年轻的矿工酒后失控，气势汹汹地拒绝买单，最后还拔出手枪威胁要打死乔。其余六个食客其实都没有看清接下来发生的情况。这个捣乱的人站在敞开的门口，手里挥舞着手枪，只见乔一闪而过，以迅雷不及掩耳之势解除了捣乱矿工的武装，把他甩到了人行道对面尘土飞扬的地上。从那时起，再也没有人愿意去与那个神秘的餐馆老板作对了。

乔的小饭馆只有六张桌子，三张在狭窄的过道两边，每张桌子都是四个座位。一位用餐者坐在一把背对着过道的椅子上，或者坐在四个长凳上的一个座位上，两个用餐者背对着背，侧面靠墙。那个穿黑衣服的人出现在乔最懒散的星期二。当他冲进屋里时，只看到一个年轻人，他吃完了东西，正在喝咖啡。他看了一眼一脸冷酷的陌生人，丢下还有半杯咖啡的杯子，快速逃离了。

乔走出厨房时，那个陌生人拖着脚绕过桌子，坐在靠北墙的长凳上。他摘下帽子，露出一头乱蓬蓬的黑发，左手穿过几天没刮的胡茬儿，盯着乔看了十秒钟，然后咆哮道："给我来一块大牛排和一些土豆条，快点。"

乔点点头，回到厨房。几分钟后，他回来了，把盘子放在他唯一的顾客面前，盘子里装满了熟透的牛排，牛排至少有一磅重，还有一大份炸土豆，还加了一碗沙拉。陌生人低头看了一会儿，然后怒视着乔。"那是大牛排吗？"他咆哮着，"把它拿走，给我一份够男人吃的。"

然后他指着沙拉。"把这个流食拿走,它不是食物。"

乔默默地把盘子和碗端回厨房。五分钟过去了,他又端了一块更大的牛排出现了,和第一块牛排一样熟,还加上一份更大的土豆。陌生人审视这份食物的时间比审视第一份食物的时间还要短。他把它推到桌子对面,眼睛眯成了一条缝。"听我说,你这条狗肉太长了。"他咆哮道。"我想要一个真正的大牛排和很多土豆,现在,既然我没有得到我点的东西,我会在你身上穿一个洞,你可以把你的胳膊放进去。"

乔再次消失了。陌生人脱下外套,放在旁边的长凳上,然后四仰八叉地靠在座位上。他知道自己是在无理取闹,但他不喜欢外国人,尤其是那些有乔这样背景的外国人,他认为自己对待细麻秆中国佬的态度很恰当,他对自己很满意。

过了十分钟,乔又端上来重做的一顿饭,这是怎样的一顿饭啊!在一个巨大的椭圆形盘子上,摆了一个长十八英寸宽十二英寸的真正巨型牛排。牛排有一英寸厚,与盘子完全重合,那块巨大的肉足足有四磅重。这有技巧的成分,因为乔把每两块大块牛排的一边都切了一下,再把其主要部分巧妙地接在一起。另一件奇怪的事情是,这一大块令人倒胃口的牛肉整个表面都呈现出菱形图案。

除了肉,乔还漫不经心地放下了一大碗土豆。当这个陌生人睁大眼睛看着食物时,乔走到门口,锁上了门,然后把卡片翻了过来,表示他的小饭馆已经打烊了——在这个时段,这可是史无前例的做法。然后他把百叶窗拉起来,遮住了门的玻璃和整个窗户。陌生人盯着这些行为。他迷惑不解,说不出话来。但是没过多久。乔就拖过一把椅子面向他,然后点点头。"你吃。"他说。

陌生人的眼睛闪闪发光。"当然,我会吃的,你这个该死的白痴。"他反驳道。"可我要像我承诺的那样,先在你身上打个洞。"他迅速伸出右手去摸枪，那把枪把不止一个男人托付给了来世——但他的速度不够快。中国人乔以魔术师的速度和灵巧，把左手伸进系长袍的腰带，摸出一把刀，刀从桌子上呼啸而过，穿过陌生人的衬衫袖子，扎进他右前臂外侧的一片布料里，砰的一声钉到松木靠背上，把陌生人的胳膊钉住了。

这个人本来可以把手臂抽出来，但是他却选择了去摸左边的手枪。乔又一次领先一步。他从腰带里摸出另一把刀，重复了他那神奇的表演。这一次，刀在陌生人的左肘内侧穿了一个洞，把陌生人的手臂钉在了长凳上。还没等那人再有动作，乔就把手伸进长袍的褶裥，掏出一把使他刚才用的那把相形见绌的另一把刀。刀刃有一英尺长，刀柄两英寸宽，是卡特勒艺术的杰出典范。转瞬间，它就逗弄得陌生人的喉咙发痒，使他没有任何机会动用两支枪了。

乔向他那吓坏了的顾客挥舞着一根食指。"你把手放在桌子上。"他说。那人顺从地挣脱袖子，把手放到了桌子上。乔手里仍然握着那把大刀，紧挨着那个人的喉咙，把叉子从桌子对面推过来。"你吃。"他又重复道。

"你怎么会指望我在刀口下吃饭？"被俘的顾客回答道，此时的他一点也不故作神勇了。

乔却不依不饶。"你用右手和叉子吃。若不吃，就会死。就现在。"

镇上的医生阿摩司·贝尔菲尔德每天都是中国人乔的第一位顾客。他的早餐从不变化，他通常在其他人出现之前就吃完饭离开了。上午六点，在乔这次，也是唯一一次提前打烊后，贝尔菲尔德来到这里，发现这个地方像往常一样对外开放。他走了进来，看见乔坐在陌生人的对面，陌生人爬了回来，背靠着长凳，闭着眼睛，张开的嘴里塞着一大块牛排。他面前的那块巨大的盘子和碗都是空的。乔指着他，朝医生所在的方向瞟了一眼。"你看看。"他说。

贝尔菲尔德给这个陌生人做了一个简短的检查，摸了摸他身体的各个部位，然后他微微点了点头，转向乔，说道："如果这两个容器在他开始吃之前是满的话，我会说这是一个明显的过度摄食的病例。不管怎样，他已经死了。乔，我的熏肉和鸡蛋怎么样了？"

A Clean Plate

Southeast California, 1879. The small town roasted in a three-figure temperature. It was late afternoon and hardly anyone had been outdoors since midday. Now a horseman appeared, coming in from due east. The main street was simply a continuation of the trail and on reaching it he rode its whole length, casting black eyes rapidly from side to side, taking in everything. At the western end of town he came to the livery stable. He left his horse there and walked back eastwards, stopping outside China Joe's little restaurant.

Pausing on the sidewalk, the stranger slapped dust from his clothing. His high-crowned hat, shirt and boots were black, the short jacket and trousers navy blue, worn shiny in several places. The only contrast to his general appearance of darkness came from the white bone handles of two thonged-down Colt. 45 revolvers. They were of the type known as Peacemakers, but the man didn't look as though that name applied to him. He entered the restaurant by flinging open the door with a force that caused it to rebound sharply from its metal stop, then backheeling it shut with a slam that shook the wooden building.

China Joe had lived in the town for six years and had become a local institution. His real name was not known to anyone but himself and nobody could now remember how the sobriquet had been dreamed up. Though his English was passable, he spoke little and never revealed anything about his background. Within a week of his arrival, he had set up his diner and started providing excellent dishes, both Chinese and American. His fare was so good that the staff of the nearby hotel often passed up their free meals and paid for what he offered. In addition to the gastronomic attractions, people liked to visit Joe's place on account of his appearance. Six-foot five and beanpole thin, he invariably wore a long, elaborate silk robe with a striking pattern in red, yellow, black and green. No matter how much time he spent in his kitchen, the splendid garment always looked immaculate.

The atmosphere in China Joe's place was quiet and soothing, as though he had imbued the structure with his own calm personality. The only disturbance had occurred a few months after his arrival, when a young miner got out of hand. With too much drink in him, he refused to pay his bill and became extremely aggressive, finally pulling out a handgun and threatening to use it on Joe. Not one of the other half-dozen patrons was able to follow with any real clarity what happened next. The troublemaker had been standing in the open doorway, waving his weapon, then there was a flicker of movement from Joe and the man was not only disarmed, but sent spinning across the sidewalk to land in the dusty street. From that point on, nobody had cared to antagonise the enigmatic restaurateur.

Joe's place had only six tables, three on either side of a narrow aisle and all designed to seat four. Diners took one of the chairs with backs to the walkway, or a space on one of four benches, two set against each side wall. The dark-clad man appeared on a Tuesday, Joe's slackest day. When he stormed in, the only other person in sight was a young man who'd eaten and was finishing his coffee. He took one look at the grim-faced newcomer, left his cup half full and scuttled out.

Joe came out of his kitchen as the stranger shuffled round a table and seated himself on a bench abutting the north wall. He took off his hat, revealing a tangle of black hair, rasped his left hand across several days' growth of stubble and stared at Joe for ten seconds, then growled: "Get me a big steak and some taters, and make it quick."

Joe nodded and returned to the kitchen. He came back a few minutes later and placed before his sole patron a plate laden with a perfectly cooked steak that weighed at least a pound, accompanied by a generous helping of fried potatoes, He also provided a bowl of salad. The stranger looked down for a moment, then glared at Joe.

"Call that a big steak?" he barked. "Take it away and bring me something man-sized." Then he pointed at the salad. "And get rid of this pap. It ain't food."

Without a word, Joe removed plate and bowl and went back into his kitchen. Five minutes elapsed, then he reappeared with an even bigger steak, as well prepared as the first one, plus a larger portion of potatoes. The stranger gave this offering less of his time than he'd devoted to the first one. Pushing it back across the table he narrowed his eyes to slits. "Listen to me, you long streak of dog meat," he snarled. "I want a real big steak and plenty of taters, cooked right. Now, if I don't get what I've ordered, I'm gonna blow a hole through you that you can put your arm in."

Joe disappeared again and the stranger took off his coat, put it beside him on the bench and sprawled back in his seat. He knew that there had been no reason to complain, but he didn't like foreigners, especially those with Joe's background, and he was satisfied that he had treated the gangling Chinese fellow in a fitting manner.

It was ten minutes before Joe came back with a replacement meal—and what a meal! On a huge oval platter, eighteen by twelve inches, reposed a truly monstrous steak. It was over an inch thick and overlapped the plate at both ends and sides. That gigantic slab of meat must have scaled four pounds. There was an element of artifice about it, for Joe had cut off one edge of each of a pair of vast steaks and deftly sown the two main parts together. Another curious thing about the gut-wrenching acreage of beef was that its whole surface showed a pattern of cross-hatching.

In addition to the meat, Joe plonked down a very large bowl of potatoes. As the man looked goggle-eyed at the food, Joe stepped over to the door, locked it and turned the reversible card to show that his place was closed—an unprecedented occurrence at that time of day. Then he pulled down the blinds to cover the glazed part of the door and the whole window. The stranger stared at these proceedings. He was mystified and speechless. But not for long. Joe took a chair facing him, then nodded at the victuals. "You eat," he said.

The stranger's eyes blazed. "Sure I'll eat, you damned idiot," he retorted. "But first I'll put a hole in you, just like I promised." His right hand flashed down to the gun that had consigned more than one man to the afterlife—but he wasn't quick enough. With the speed and dexterity of a conjurer, China Joe dropped his left hand into the sash he wore to secure his robe and drew out a knife, which he sent whizzing across the table. It passed through the stranger's shirt sleeve, took a sliver of the outside of his right forearm with it, and thunked into the pine backrest, pinning the limb.

The man could have freed the arm but chose instead to go for his left-side gun. Joe was ahead of him again. Producing another knife from his sash, he repeated his quasi-magical performance.

This time the weapon made a groove in the inside of the stranger's left elbow and fastened that arm to the bench, too. Before the man could make any further move, Joe delved into the folds of his robe and pulled out a knife that dwarfed the pair he had just used. With a blade over a foot long and more than two inches wide at the hilt, it was a superb example of the cutler's art. In a flash it was tickling the stranger's throat, leaving him without the slightest chance of getting either of his guns into action.

Joe flicked a forefinger at his by now very frightened patron. "You put hands on table," he said. The man pulled his sleeves free and complied. Still holding the big knife close to the man's throat, Joe pushed a fork across the table. "You eat," he said again.

"How the hell do you expect me to do that with a blade at my gizzard?" the captive customer replied, all bravado having deserted him.

Joe was inexorable. "You use right hand and fork. You not eat, you die. Now."

The town doctor, Amos Belfield, was always China Joe's first customer of the day. His breakfast never varied and he had usually eaten and left before anyone else turned up. At six in the morning after Joe's one and only early closure, Belfield arrived to find the place apparently open for business as usual. He walked in and saw Joe sitting opposite the stranger, who was sprawled back against the bench with his eyes closed and a large lump of steak in his open mouth. The enormous plate and the bowl in front of him were both empty. Joe pointed at him and glanced in the doctor's direction. "You look-see," he said.

Belfield carried out a brief examination of the stranger, feeling various parts of his body, then he nodded curtly and turned to Joe. "If those two pieces of crockery were full when he started eating, I'd say this is a clear case of over-ingestion. Anyway, he's dead. Now, what about my bacon and eggs, Joe?"

丑 女

格洛里亚确实有值得关注的地方。也许是她浓密的金发、漂亮的肤色、娇嫩的皮肤、姣好的身材,或者是她任何时候都知道她的身体的所有部位在哪里。

也许是因为她长得丑。

但是她身上有一种神奇的东西,这种东西超越了鲨鱼渔夫被大白鲨包围时眼里闪烁的光芒,有些东西,超越了天上无穷无尽的繁星。

也许格洛里亚的内在本质会在有露的清晨在一朵白玫瑰上闪亮。

也许这是看不见的。

一天,她被同学嘲笑,回家后哭了。

她母亲坐下来说:"格洛里亚,你真漂亮。我不是指内在,因为每个人的内在都很丑。你前额凸出,两眼的眼距惊人,鼻子曲线玲珑,还是歪的,嘴巴曲线动人。上帝对你很好。好看的人似乎都一样,因为他们五官平平。格洛里亚,你非同寻常,你的容貌与众不同。你很漂亮,你的外表美只是你如此与众不同的一部分。"

"我们死定了吗,妈妈?"

"只要你醒悟过来就可以。像所有有天赋的人一样,你必须付出代价。只有把你的天赋告诉别人,把他们内心的丑陋暴露出来,他们才会知道你有多美。"

几年后，在她十八岁生日的时候，格洛里亚和乔叔叔一起吃午饭。

"格洛里亚，你的嘴真漂亮。"

格洛里亚唠叨着。"哦，天哪。你们这些家伙总是这样信口胡言吗？"

"不。"他厉声说。"你是个漂亮的女孩。当然，像每个人一样，我必须摆脱内心的丑陋，才能看到你的美丽，但是我现在看到了。你今天十八岁了，现在是你去当地酒吧选一个男人的时候了。"

那天晚上，格洛里亚走进当地一家酒吧，大步走向她看到的最漂亮的男人。他看上去很沮丧，但她觉得这激起了自己的挑战心理。

她坐在他旁边说："嗨，我叫格洛里亚。你叫什么名字？"

"拉尔夫。"他忧郁地说。

"一个大小伙子，干吗这么沮丧？要不要我请你喝一杯？"

他转过身来，眼睛睁得大大的。"好吧，但你不是我喜欢的类型。"

当他们的饮料送过来的时候，她微笑着说："看着我，拉尔夫。我很漂亮。"

"不行，亲爱的。你是我见过的最丑的女孩。"

格洛里亚并没有畏缩，而是开心地啜饮着饮料，像春天的青蛙一样快乐。"我有一种特别的美，拉尔夫。"如果她那么丑，为什么一个英俊的男人会这样看着她？

"我不是指内在。每个人的内心都很丑陋。我是说外表。但是为了看到我的美丽，你必须摆脱你内心的丑陋。"

拉尔夫叹了口气。"不行，亲爱的。你需要整形手术。"

格洛里亚第一次尝到酒的味道，她把浓密的金发甩了甩。"何必费那个事呢？我像我一样美丽，对我来说够了。你为什么这么沮丧啊？"

他抱怨说："我昨晚失眠了。"他回头看了一眼穿红裤子的金发女郎，她正笑着抓住一个年轻人的胳膊。"看见那个女孩了吗？昨晚我去她家赴约,却看见她上了另一个男人的车扬长而去。有三个人因为她自杀过。"

格洛里亚扮了个鬼脸。"为什么,拉尔夫?她看起来很普通。"

拉尔夫咳嗽了一声。"普通?她可以得到她想要的任何男人。"

"瞎说吧,拉尔夫?她看起来很漂亮,因为她五官平平。"

金发女郎慢悠悠地走了过来,搂着拉尔夫。"对不起,拉尔夫。我忘了我已经和另一个人约好了,我们明天晚上再约吧。"

"不用了,谢谢。我已经和这个女孩有约了。"

金发女郎看着格洛里亚,怒气冲冲地说,"你不可能和这样的女孩约会。"

拉尔夫把饮料一饮而尽。"是真的。"

"你真恶心。那就算了吧。只要我想,像你这样的男人我随时一抓一大把。"

她离开了,但眼睛却一直没有离开拉尔夫。格洛里亚捂住了嘴,逗得他哈哈大笑。"看见了吗?她是内外都丑陋。我们到你家去吧。"

拉尔夫笑了。"你这么天真啊?"

"我可能是天真,拉尔夫,但我有特殊的能力。我有一种本能。我随时都知道自己身体各个部位所在的位置。"

拉尔夫眨眼。"所以呢?"

"这种本能需要肌肉、神经、骨骼和脑细胞的不可思议的整合,真是太神奇啦!你看。"

金发女郎正和她的新同伴走过来,让拉尔夫心生嫉妒,格洛里亚挥动双臂,拍了拍金发女郎的后背。她东倒西歪地走着,格洛里亚试图扶她起来,却被她打了一巴掌,走开了。

"格洛里亚，"拉尔夫说，"我现在看到你的美了。"

"真的，拉尔夫。与你的价值相比，你的困难似乎更多。"

"但是我需要你，格洛里亚。我现在能看到你的美了。"

格洛里亚双手抱胸。"算了吧，拉尔夫。我刚才撒了谎。我真的很丑。不信你问问这个房间里的任何人。"

"嘿，请问大家，这个女孩丑吗？"

"不丑！"他们异口同声地大叫。

"听，格洛里亚。你很漂亮。幸亏有了你，这里的每个人内心现在都没那么丑陋了。"

格洛里亚凝视着他恳求的目光。"好吧，我们走吧。我希望你有公寓。"

拉尔夫跟哪个幼嫩光滑的美女都没有过这么多的乐趣。早上，他跑到浴室里呕吐，但那是因为喝得太多了，格洛里亚用番茄汁和塔巴斯科调味汁调配起来给他喝。那天晚些时候，他从公寓的窗户向外望去，看见码头上吊着一条鲨鱼。

"我想当一个捕鲨渔民。"他说。

他当上了。格洛里亚成了一名护士。他们一个月后结婚了。

两年后，格洛里亚来到船甲板上照镜子。"我不知道。也许我应该做个整形手术。"

"何必费那个事儿呢？"拉尔夫边说边拉上来一条虎鲨。"你这样就很美。"

故事的经过就是这样。

The Ugly Girl

There was something about Gloria. Maybe it was her thick, blond hair, nice skin tone, nice body, or that she knew where all her body parts were at any moment.

Maybe it was that she was ugly.

But something was magical about her, something beyond the gleam in eyes of a shark fisherman surrounded by great whites, something beyond the infinity of the stars above.

Perhaps Gloria's essence could be seen glistening on a white rose on a dewy morning.

Perhaps it couldn't be seen.

One day, she came home crying after being teased by her classmates.

Her mother sat her down and said, "Gloria, you're beautiful. I don't mean inside, because everybody is ugly inside. You have a prominent forehead, startling wide-apart eyes, an exquisite curved and twisted nose, and an electrifying crooked mouth. God has been good to you. Good looking people only seem that way because they have average features. And, Gloria, you're not at all average.

You have distinctive looks. You're gorgeous, and your physical beauty is only part of what makes you so special."

"Are we done yet, Mom?"

"Not until you come to your senses. Like all gifted people, you must pay a price. Only by telling people of your gifts and bringing out their ugliness inside will they see how beautiful you are."

Years later, on her eighteenth birthday, Gloria ate lunch with Uncle Joe.

"You have a beautiful mouth, Gloria."

Gloria gagged. "Oh, god. Don't you guys ever let up on that crap?"

"No," he snapped. "You're a beautiful girl. Sure, like everyone, I had to rid myself of my ugliness inside to see your beauty, but I see it now. You're eighteen today. It's time for you to go to a local bar and pick up a man."

That night, Gloria marched into a local bar and strode up to the best looking guy she saw. He looked depressed, but she felt inspired by the challenge.

She sat beside him and said, "Hi, I'm Gloria. What's your name?"

"Ralph," he said in his gloom.

"Why so down big fella? How about I buy you a drink?"

He turned and his eyes blasted open. "All right, but you're not my type."

When their drinks arrived, she smiled and said, "Look at me, Ralph. I'm gorgeous."

"No way, honey. You're the ugliest girl I've ever met."

Undeterred, Gloria delightedly sipped her drink, as happy as a frog in springtime. "I have a special kind of beauty, Ralph." If she was so ugly, why was a handsome man looking her way?

"I don't mean inside. Everyone is ugly inside. I mean outside. But to see my beauty, you must rid yourself of the ugliness inside you."

Ralph sighed. "No way, honey. You need plastic surgery."

Reeling from her first taste of liquor, Gloria tossed her thick blond hair. "Why bother. I'm beautiful like I am. Enough about me. Why are you so depressed?"

He groaned. "I got stood up last night." He glanced back at a flashy blond in red slacks, laughing and clutching the arm of a young man. "See that girl? When I got to her house for our date last night, I saw her get in another guy's car and ride off. Three guys have attempted suicide because of her."

Gloria grimaced. "Why, Ralph? She's so average looking."

Ralph coughed. "Average? She can get any guy she wants."

"Nonsense, Ralph? She only seems beautiful because of her average features."

The blond sauntered over and slid her arm around Ralph.

"Sorry, Ralph. I forgot I'd already made a date with another guy. Let's make it for tomorrow night."

"No thanks. I already have a date with this girl."

The blond looked at Gloria and huffed. "There's no way you'd date a girl like that."

Ralph swallowed his drink. "Believe it."

"You're disgusting. Forget it then. I walk over guys like you anytime I want."

She left, but kept her eyes on Ralph. Gloria gagged and made him laugh. "See? She's ugly inside and out. Let's go to your place."

Ralph laughed. "You are so naive?"

"I may be naive, Ralph, but I have special abilities. I have proprioception. I know the position of all my body parts at any moment."

Ralph blinked. "So?"

"Proprioception takes an incredible integration of muscles, nerves, bones, and brain cells. It's amazing. Look."

Gloria swung her arms and smacked with her backswing the blonde, who was walking by with her new companion to make Ralph jealous. She went sprawling, and Gloria tried to help her up, but she slapped her away and marched off.

"Gloria," said Ralph, "I see your beauty now."

"Really, Ralph. You seem more trouble than you're worth."

"But I want you, Gloria. I can see your beauty now."

Gloria folded her arms. "Forget it, Ralph. I was lying. I'm really ugly. Ask any guy in this room."

"Hey, everyone, is this girl ugly?"

"No!" they all yelled.

"See, Gloria. You're beautiful. Everyone here has less ugliness inside thanks to you."

Gloria gazed at his pleading eyes. "All right, let's go. I hope you have condominiums."

Ralph never had so much fun with any girl as he did with the slipping and sliding beauty. In the morning, he ran to the bathroom to throw up, but it was from drinking too much, and Gloria fixed him with a tomato juice and Tabasco sauce concoction. Later that day, he looked out his condominium window and saw a shark hanging by a dock.

"I want to be a shark fisherman," he said.

And he did. And Gloria became a nurse. And they got married a month later.

Two years later, Gloria came out on the boat deck looking in a mirror. "I don't know. Maybe I should have plastic surgery."

"Why bother," said Ralph, pulling in a tiger shark. "You're beautiful the way you are."

And that was that.

选一种姿态　让自己活得无可替代

勒赎信

［美国］明德雷特·洛德

鲍比·斯科特被绑架，三天后来了信。收信人写的是"R.斯科特亲启"。盖着纽约的邮戳。

"可能是绑架者寄来的。"美国联邦调查局负责本案的埃文斯说。他万分小心地打开信封，用镊子夹出了两页纸，在书桌上展开。两页纸都是用铅笔写的，一页是印刷体，一页是鲍比手写的。

第一页纸写的是：

如果你还想见到你的孩子，就准备好十万美元的小额纸币。

男孩的信上写的是：

亲爱的爸爸：

他们说我应该给您写封信报个平安，因为这样就能证明我没死。为了证明真是我写的信，我就给您描写一下小鸟吧。我看见一只鸟在啄一棵树，这只鸟除了头和脖子是白色的，全身都是黑色。在小鸟的头的后面有一个红色小斑点。还有一只鸟，是一种麻雀，只有它在唱歌，鸟的头顶是灰色的，从上到下都有黑色条纹，尾巴非常短。我扔了一根树枝，鸟就向南飞去，我敢说它一口气能飞十英里。这里还有一只蓝知更鸟，发出咯咯响的噪声。好吧，希望很快见到您。

爱你的鲍比

美国联邦调查局负责此案的埃文斯看了看桌上摆放的男孩的照片，男孩身体强壮结实。"这个孩子很爱大自然，对吧？好啦，我检查一下这些信上的指纹，说不定能得到一点线索。"

斯科特先生摇摇头。"是的，他一直爱好研究鸟类。可是，你瞧，这封信里有一些错误。我抄一份行吗？"他抄写完信，拿起帽子向外走。"我到图书馆去一下，我去去就回。"

两个小时以后，斯科特先生回来了。埃文斯没有什么可报告的。他没有从那些信上得到任何线索，没有指纹，什么都找不到。

斯科特说："看这里，埃文斯。你没找到什么，而我倒是有种预感。不只是预感，我相信是事实。你会认为我疯了。也许我就是疯了，但是我要坐飞机去加利福尼亚州，现在就去！"

"加利福尼亚州！可是邮戳是纽约的啊。"埃文斯开始争辩。他接着问道："你了解什么我不知道的东西吧？究竟是什么意思呢？"

"还不敢肯定。你尽管相信我好了，要是你不想跟我去，我就自己去。"

当他们在加利福尼亚州的圣巴巴拉市下飞机时，一队警务人员在等着他们。

斯科特告诉他们："我要找的地方距离这里以北约十英里远，那里是长着高大松树的田野，附近不是有一条溪流就是有一个小湖。我从没见过那个地方,但是我十分肯定就在那里。"

一个警员说:"说得对,确实在那里,几年前我曾经到那个方向搜索过。"

他们没费周折就找到那里。隐藏的地点只能有一处,那是一幢多年都没人住过的旧木屋。警察从三面包围上去,没费一枪一弹就捉住了被惊得目瞪口呆的守卫。

斯科特把儿子抱在怀里,埃文斯听见男孩说:"我就知道你会来,爸爸。我知道你会明白的。"

美国联邦调查局的埃文斯抱怨道:"我一直蒙在鼓里,现在说说整个经过吧。我猜正是你儿子的信指引你找到他的,可到底是怎么回事呢?"

斯科特先生哈哈大笑,拍了拍鲍勃的肩头,说:"没什么神秘的地方,那封信让人觉得像是以前从未见过鸟的人写的,但是鲍勃研究鸟类已经有好几年的时间,他认识所有的鸟。起初我不明白为什么他假装那么笨,实际上他写得非常聪明。"

"真见鬼。"男孩说。"咱们走吧。"

斯科特先生接着说:"我在图书馆查到鲍勃信里写的鸟,发现了答案。他说的白头啄木鸟属于太平洋沿岸的松林地区,他描述的唱歌麻雀叫作'圣巴巴拉麻雀',只有一种蓝知更鸟叫起来咯咯响,叫作鱼狗,总是离淡水不远。"

"真是,这下我全明白了。"埃文斯说。"但是离圣巴巴拉市约十英里,这是怎么回事?"

斯科特先生笑着说:"那主要是我猜出来的。鲍勃信上说那只麻雀可以向南飞十英里,中间不停。我知道麻雀只作短途飞行,从一棵树上飞到另一棵树上。等我开始明白鲍勃在巧妙地告诉我们他在什么地方时,一切都严丝合缝地对接起来了。"

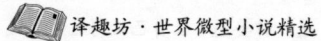

Ransom Note

By Mindret Lord

The letter came the third day after Bobby Scott was kidnapped. It was addressed "R. Scott—Personal." The postmark was New York.

"This maybe it," said Evans, the FBI man on the case. He opened the envelope with great care. With a pair of tweezers he took out two sheets of paper. He spread them out on the desk. Both were written in pencil. One was printed. The other was in Bobby's handwriting.

The first sheet read:

IF YOU WANT TO SEE YOUR KID AGAIN HAVE $100,000 READY IN SMALL BILLS.

The boy's letter was:

Dear Dad: They said I should write you that I am okay

because that would prove I am not dead. So I will write you about birds to prove this is really me. One bird I saw was pecking a tree. It was all black except for a white head and neck. It had a little red patch on the back of its head. There was another bird—sort of a sparrow—only it sings. It was gray on top with black streaks above and below. It had a very short tail. When I threw a stick it flew away south, and I bet it didn't stop for ten miles. There is a bluebird around here too that makes a noise like a rattle. Well, hope to see you soon.

Love, Bob.

The FBI man looked at the picture of the husky boy that stood on the desk. "The kid's quite a nature lover, isn't he? Well, I'll check these letters for fingerprints. Maybe that will give us a clue."

Mr. Scott was shaking his head. "Yes, bird study has always been his hobby. But—you know—there's something wrong about this letter. Let me make a copy of it, will you?" When he finished, he picked up his hat and started out. "I'm going to the library for a while. I'll be back soon."

Two hours later Mr. Scott came back. The FBI man had nothing to report. The letters had given him no clues. There were no fingerprints—nothing to go on.

Scott said, "Look here, Evans. You don't have anything, but I have a hunch. It's more than a hunch. I believe it. You might think I'm crazy. Maybe I am. But I'm flying to California—right now!"

"California! But the postmark was New York," Evans started to argue. Then he asked, "Do you know something I don't? What is this all about anyway?"

"Nothing sure. You've just got to trust me. If you won't come with me, I'll go alone."

A group of men from the sheriff's office was waiting for them when they landed in Santa Barbara, California.

"The place I'm looking for," Scott told them, "would be about ten miles north of here. It's in high pine country, and it's near either a stream or a small lake. I've never seen the place. But I'm pretty sure it's there."

"Sure," said one of the men. "It's there all right. I used to hunt up that way years ago."

They found the place with no trouble. There was only one possible hide-out—an old cabin that no one had used for years. The officers came up to it from three sides. They were able to take the surprised guards without firing shot.

Scott took his son in his arms. Evans heard the boy say, "I knew you'd come, Dad. I knew you could figure it out."

"I've played dumb long enough," the FBI man complained. "Let's have the whole story now. I've guessed that your son's letter led you right to him. But how?"

Mr. Scott laughed and patted Bob on the shoulder. "It's not much of a secret," he said. "That letter sounded like it had been written by someone who had never seen a bird before. But Bob has studied birds for years. He knows all about them. At first I couldn't figure out why he was pretending to be so stupid. It was really pretty smart."

"Aw heck," the boy said. "Let's go."

Mr. Scott went on. "I found the answer in the library when I checked on the birds Bob wrote about in his letter. The white-headed woodpecker he told about belongs in the pine country on the Pacific coast. The song sparrow he described is known as the 'Santa Barbara sparrow.' There is only one bluebird that has a cry like a rattle—the kingfisher. And he is never far from fresh water."

"Yes, I can see all that," Evans said. "But how about the ten miles from Santa Barbara?"

"I guessed that much by myself," Mr. Scott laughed. "Bob said in his letter the sparrow flew south and didn't stop for ten miles. I know sparrows only make short flights—from tree to tree. When I began to understand that Bob was smart enough to let us know where he was, everything fitted together."

"贫穷是什么？"

[美国] 乔·古德温·帕克

你问我贫穷是什么？听我说，我就站在这里，肮脏不堪，气味难闻，没有"合适的"衬衣穿，腐蛀的牙齿臭不可闻。我会告诉你，听我说，不要带着怜悯听，我不想利用你的怜悯。带着理解听，设身处地地想象我肮脏、破烂、不适宜的境遇，听我说。

贫穷是每天早晨从沾有灰尘和病人污迹的垫子上爬起来，床单兼做尿布已有多年。贫穷就是生活在一种挥之不去的味道中：尿味、酸牛奶味，还有腐烂的食物和烧煳的洋葱的刺鼻味道的混合味。洋葱便宜。就算你闻过这味道，你也不会晓得这味道是怎么来的。那是户外厕所的味道。那是小孩子不敢在夜里走漆黑的长路，尿床所造成的味道。那是牛奶变酸的味道，因为冰箱已经失修良久，而修理需要金钱。我可以把垃圾掩埋，而铁锹何处寻？铁锹要花钱买呀。

贫穷是疲惫不堪。我一直都感到疲惫不堪。我最小的那个孩子出生的时候，医院的医生告诉我，我患有因营养不良以及严重的寄生虫病引发的慢性贫血，需要进行整治手术。我礼貌地听着——穷人总是礼貌的，穷人永远在洗耳恭听。他们不说我没钱买补铁剂、更好的食物以及驱虫剂。我一想到手术就害怕，手术费用如此昂贵，以至于我如果真做手术的话，我会哈哈大笑的。术后恢复需要很长时间，三个孩子托付何人？我最后一次工作时，把孩子交给"奶奶"看管，结果回家后发现婴儿浑身都是苍蝇屎，尿布还是原来那块。为孩子换那块已经干了的尿布时，一片片皮肉也被带了下来。另一个孩子在玩玻璃碴。最大的孩子独自一人在湖边玩耍。我一个星期挣二十二美元，而这三个孩子上一个像样的托儿所需要二十美元，于是我辞掉了工作。

贫穷是肮脏。你身穿洁净的衣服从洁净的家里走出，你可以说"每个人都可以干净呀"。让我来说明一下没钱是怎么过日子的。早餐我给孩子吃不带黄油的面包渣，或者不带鸡蛋、黄油的玉米面包，这样就能少用盘子。不管是什么盘子，我只用冷水洗，而且不用肥皂，即使是最便宜的肥皂也要省下来洗尿布。你看看我这双手，这么红肿、干裂。有一次，我省吃俭用了两个月，只想买瓶凡士林涂手，治疗孩子身上因尿布引起的皮疹。等到我终于把钱攒够了，却发现价格又涨了两美分，我和婴儿还要继续忍受下去。我不得不每天都面临这选择：是否还受得了把红肿干裂的手伸进冷水里，接触刺激性很强的肥皂。可你又要问了，为什么不用热水呢？买燃料要花钱，买木炭要花钱。热水是奢侈品，我用不起奢侈品。如果我告诉你我多年轻，你一定会惊讶的，因为我看起来要比实际年龄老相得多。我每天弯腰曲背地在水池前洗那么长时间，以至于都记不清自己还做过其他事情。我晚上给上学了的女儿洗那几件衣服，只盼望她的衣服第二天早晨能干。

贫穷是在寒夜里整夜守着的味道，要盯着炉子里的火，假如有一粒火星落到用报纸糊的墙上，熟睡的婴儿就会葬身火海。在夏季，贫穷就是看护婴儿，防止他哭泣时流下的眼泪被小虫子和苍蝇吞食。纱窗都烂了，你知道自己付的房租太少，所以永远也不会有人来修。贫穷意味着虫子在你的食物、鼻子和眼睛里出现，你睡觉时在你的身上爬。贫穷就是期待永远都不要下雨,因为只要一下雨,尿布就不会干,你很快就得用报纸替代尿布。贫穷就是看着你的孩子永远流着鼻涕,纸巾要用钱来买,而所有的破布都另有用途。抗组胺药就更贵了。贫穷是无米炊和无皂洗涤。

贫穷就是哀告求助。你可曾有过哀告求助的经历,心里明白如果得不到帮助,孩子就要受苦?考虑一下向亲戚借钱吧,如果这是你能想象的唯一求助方式。我会告诉你哀告求助是什么滋味。你找到你想要去的办公室的位置。你在那个街区绕了四五圈,想到孩子,你终于硬着头皮走了进去。人人都很忙。最后有人走出来,你说你需要帮助,而那个人却绝对不是你想要见的人。在把自己贫困的窘境向坐在对面办公桌后面的人和盘托出后,你发现这根本不是你要找的办公室——也就是说,你必须把这个过程从头到尾再重复一遍,而在下一处再说一遍同样艰难。

你是来求助的,说到底是要付出代价的。人家再次告诉你要等待,人家还告诉了你要等待的原因,可是你被羞愧和越来越强烈的绝望阴影所笼罩,因此实际上什么也没听见。

贫穷是回忆。我还记得上初中时衣衫褴褛,全身异味,遭到"好"孩子的无情打击而逃学。校纪检察官到家里来了,母亲告诉他我怀孕了,尽管我并没有怀孕。她想我可以找份工作帮大人养家糊口。我干干停停,每次时间都不够,所以没能学会一门手艺。我记得最清楚的是出嫁的时候,那时我是多么年轻。我现在也还年轻。曾有一度,我们拥有你现在所拥有的一切。我们在另一个小镇也曾拥有一幢带热水及其他设施的房子。后来,我丈夫失业了,开始还有失业救济金,我也能找到那么几份工作。然而不久,我们所有的好东西都被没收了,人也被迫搬回这里来。我当时已经有孕在身。我们刚刚搬进来时,这幢房子看起来还不太糟糕。随后,房子的状况每况愈下,什么设施都没有维修过。我们当时没有钱,丈夫偶尔能找到几份零工，可跟现在一样，工钱都花在吃的上面了。直到现在我都弄不明白，我们当时带着三个婴儿是怎么熬过那三年的，可事实上我们确实熬过来了。我要告诉你点儿事，我最小的孩子出生以后，我亲手毁了这桩婚姻。这桩婚姻也曾是一桩美满的婚姻，可是，你还能继续在这种肮脏的环境中生儿育女吗？你是否想过任何节育措施都要花费很多钱？丈夫离去那天，我心里明白，但我们没有说再见。我只盼望他能摆脱这种困境，但是如果有我们的拖累，他永远不会有希望。

我就是这时求助的。等我得到了救济，你知道是多少钱吗？当时、现在都一样，我们一家四口每月七十八美元，那就是我曾经得到的全部。现在你明白我们没有肥皂、没有热水、没有阿司匹林、没有驱虫药、没有护手霜、没有洗发香波的原因了吧？这些东西永远永远不会有了，一样也不会有了。这样，你就很清楚了，每月我用二十美元付房租，剩下的钱全部用来买全家四口的口粮，买面包渣和玉米面包，以及米、牛奶和豆子。我尽可能地把用电量减少到最小，因为假如超出一点点，饭就得少吃了。

贫穷就是前途黑暗。你的孩子不会与我的孩子嬉戏，我儿子只能与偷儿为伴。我似乎已经看到了我的孩子在铁窗栏杆后面，而不是贫穷栏杆后面的样子。或者，他们会转向酒精和毒品寻求解脱，但最终会发现反受其累。而我的女儿会怎么样？她充其量也就像我这样苟活着。

可是，你却可能对我说，孩子可以上学嘛。没错儿，可以上学。可我的孩子没有课外书，没有杂志，没有铅笔和蜡笔，没有纸，更重要的是，他们没有健康的身体。他们身上有虫子，他们有传染病，他们整个夏天眼睛都是红红的，他们在地板上睡不好，跟我挤在唯一的一张床上也睡不好。他们没饿着，我那七十八美元可以保证他们饿不死，但他们确实营养不良。哦，是的，我确实还记得在校时所学的有关健康的知识，但这派不上多大用场。有些地方有额外商品计划，可是这里没有，国家声称该计划耗资巨大。学校有午餐计划，可是，等我的孩子上学时，他们的健康早就毁了。

可是你对我说，有卫生诊所啊。没错儿，可卫生诊所都在城里，我的住处在这里，距离城里有八英里的路程。虽然来回要十六英里，我可以步行那么远，可我那年幼的孩子能吗？我的邻居去城里时可以把我们捎上，可是他却希望这样或者那样的回报。我打赌你是了解我的邻居的，他就是那种身材高大，把时间花在加油站、理发店，并且在街角店里抱怨政府在私生子的不道德的母亲身上花钱太多的人。

贫穷是一种酸性物质，能一点点地腐蚀人的自尊，使其荡然无存。贫穷是一把凿子，它能削切尊严，使其消失殆尽。你们中间有人说，如果你们处在我的境遇里，你们会做点事。也许你们能做义工一个星期或者一个月，可你们能年复一年地坚持下去吗？

穷人也有梦想，梦想着有一天有钱，有钱买合适的食物，买驱虫剂，买补铁剂，买牙刷，买护手霜，买一把锤子、一点儿钉子和一小片儿窗纱，买一把铁锹，买一点儿油漆，买几块床单，买针线，还有去城里的车费。还有，哦，有钱买热水，有钱买肥皂。梦想求助不会吞噬最后的那点儿自尊。你所去的办公室与政府的其他办事处一样好，那里有足够的工作人员，能够快速为你提供帮助，工作人员不会因失败和绝望而离职。当你不得不把自己的故事讲出来的时候，只讲给一个人听，而那个人可以为你提供其他帮助，这样你就不用一次又一次地证实自己的贫穷了。

我是以出离愤怒的态度告诉你这些的。记住，你和我生活在同一时空，你的周围到处都有我的同类。义愤填膺地看待我们吧，义愤对你帮助我会有好处，义愤会促使你讲述我的故事。穷人总是默默无言，而你还能缄默依旧吗？

"What Is Poverty?"

By Jo Goodwin Parker

You ask me what is poverty? Listen to me. Here I am, dirty, smelly, and with no "proper" underwear on and with the stench of my rotting teeth near you. I will tell you. Listen to me. Listen without pity. I cannot use your pity. Listen with understanding. Put yourself in my dirty, worn-out, ill-fitting shoes, and hear me.

Poverty is getting up every morning from a dirt- and illness-stained mattress. The sheets have long since been used for diapers. Poverty is living in a smell that never leaves. This is a smell of urine, sour milk, and spoiling food sometimes joined with the strong smell of long-cooked onions. Onions are cheap. If you have smelled this smell, you did not know how it came. It is the smell of the outdoor privy. It is the smell of young children who cannot walk the long dark way in the night. It is the smell of the mattresses where years of "accidents" have happened. It is the smell of the milk which has gone sour because the refrigerator long has not worked, and it costs money to get it fixed. It is the smell of rotting garbage. I could bury it, but where is the shovel? Shovels cost money.

  Poverty is being tired. I have always been tired. They told me at the hospital when the last baby came that I had chronic anemia caused from poor diet, a bad case of worms, and that I needed a corrective operation. I listened politely—the poor are always polite. The poor always listen. They don't say that there is no money for iron pills, or better food, or worm medicine. The idea of an operation is frightening and costs so much that, if I had dared, I would have laughed. Who takes care of my children? Recovery from an operation takes a long time. I have three children. When I left them with "Granny" the last time I had a job, I came home to find the baby covered with fly specks, and a diaper that had not been changed since I left. When the dried diaper came off, bits of my baby's flesh came with it. My other child was playing with a sharp bit of broken glass, and my oldest was playing alone at the edge of a lake. I made twenty-two dollars a week, and a good nursery school costs twenty dollars a week for three children. I quit my job.

  Poverty is dirt. You can say in your clean clothes coming from your clean house, "Anybody can be clean." Let me explain about housekeeping with no money. For breakfast I give my children grits with no oleo or cornbread without eggs and oleo. This does not use up many dishes. What dishes there are, I wash in cold water and with no soap. Even the cheapest soap has to be saved for the baby's diapers. Look at my hands, so cracked and red. Once I saved for two months to buy a jar of Vaseline for my hands and the baby's diaper rash. When I had saved enough, I went to buy it and the price had gone up two cents. The baby and I suffered on. I have to decide every day if I can bear to put my cracked sore hands into the cold water and strong soap. But you ask, why not hot water? Fuel costs money. If you have a wood fire, it costs money. If you burn electricity, it costs money. Hot water is a luxury. I do not have luxuries. I know you will be surprised when I tell you how young I am. I look so much older. My back has been bent over the wash tubs every day for so long, I cannot remember when I ever did anything else. Every night I wash every stitch my school age child has on and just hope her clothes will be dry by morning.

Poverty is staying up all night on cold nights to watch the fire knowing one spark on the newspaper covering the walls means your sleeping child dies in flames. In summer poverty is watching gnats and flies devour your baby's tears when he cries. The screens are torn and you pay so little rent you know they will never be fixed. Poverty means insects in your food, in your nose, in your eyes, and crawling over you when you sleep. Poverty is hoping it never rains because diapers won't dry when it rains and soon you are using newspapers. Poverty is seeing your children forever with runny noses. Paper handkerchiefs cost money and all your rags you need for other things. Even more costly are antihistamines. Poverty is cooking without food and cleaning without soap.

Poverty is asking for help. Have you ever had to ask for help, knowing your children will suffer unless you get it? Think about asking for a loan from a relative, if this is the only way you can imagine asking for help. I will tell you how it feels. You find out where the office is that you are supposed to visit. You circle that block four or five times. Thinking of your children, you go in. Everyone is very busy. Finally, someone comes out and you tell her that you need help. That never is the person you need to see. You go see another person, and after spilling the whole shame of your poverty all over the desk between you, you find that this isn't the right office after all—you must repeat the whole process, and it never is any easier at the next place.

You have asked for help, and after all it has a cost. You are again told to wait. You are told why, but you don't really hear because of the red cloud of shame and the rising cloud of despair.

Poverty is remembering. It is remembering quitting school in junior high because "nice" children had been so cruel about my clothes and my smell. The attendance officer came. My mother told him I was pregnant. I wasn't, but she thought that I could get a job and help out. I had jobs off and on, but never long enough to learn anything. Mostly I remember being married. I was so young then. I am still young. For a time, we had all the things you have. There was a little house in another town, with hot water and everything. Then my husband lost his job. There was unemployment insurance for a while and what few jobs I could get. Soon, all our nice things were repossessed and we moved back here. I was pregnant then. This house didn't look so bad when we first moved in. Every week it gets worse. Nothing is ever fixed. We now had no money. There were a few odd jobs for my husband, but everything went for food then, as it does now. I don't know how we lived through three years and three babies, but we did. I'll tell you something, after the last baby I destroyed my marriage. It had been a good one, but could you keep on bringing children in this dirt? Did you ever think how much it costs for any kind of birth control? I knew my husband was leaving the day he left, but there were no goodbye between us. I hope he has been able to climb out of this mess somewhere. He never could hope with us to drag him down.

That's when I asked for help. When I got it, you know how much it was? It was, and is, seventy-eight dollars a month for the four of us; that is all I ever can get. Now you know why there is no soap, no needles and thread, no hot water, no aspirin, no worm medicine, no hand cream, no shampoo. None of these things forever and ever and ever. So that you can see clearly, I pay twenty dollars a month rent, and most of the rest goes for food. For grits and cornmeal, and rice and milk and beans. I try my best to use only the minimum electricity. If I use more, there is that much less for food.

Poverty is looking into a black future. Your children won't play with my boys. They will turn to other boys who steal to get what they want. I can already see them behind the bars of their prison instead of behind the bars of my poverty. Or they will turn to the freedom of alcohol or drugs, and find themselves enslaved. And my daughter? At best, there is for her a life like mine.

But you say to me, there are schools. Yes, there are schools. My children have no extra books, no magazines, no extra pencils, or crayons, or paper and most important of all, they do not have health. They have worms, they have infections, they have pink-eye all summer. They do not sleep well on the floor, or with me in my one bed. They do not suffer from hunger, my seventy-eight dollars keeps us alive, but they do suffer from malnutrition. Oh yes, I do remember what I was taught about health in school. It doesn't do much good. In some places there is a surplus commodities program. Not here. The country said it cost too much. There is a school lunch program. But I have two children who will already be damaged by the time they get to school.

But, you say to me, there are health clinics. Yes, there are health clinics and they are in the towns. I live out here eight miles from town. I can walk that far (even if it is sixteen miles both ways), but can my little children? My neighbor will take me when he goes; but he expects to get paid, one way or another. I bet you know my neighbor. He is that large man who spends his time at the gas station, the barbershop, and the corner store complaining about the government spending money on the immoral mothers of illegitimate children.

Poverty is an acid that drips on pride until all pride is worn away. Poverty is a chisel that chips on honor until honor is worn away. Some of you say that you would do something in my situation, and maybe you would, for the first week or the first month, but for year after year after year?

Even the poor can dream. A dream of a time when there is money. Money for the right kinds of food, for worm medicine, for iron pills, for toothbrushes, for hand cream, for a hammer and nails and a bit of screening, for a shovel, for a bit of paint, for some sheeting, for needles and thread. Money to pay in money for a trip to town. And, oh, money for hot water and money for soap. A dream of when asking for help does not eat away the last bit of pride. When the office you visit is as nice as the offices of other governmental agencies, when there are enough workers to help you quickly, when workers do not quit in defeat and despair. When you have to tell your story to only one person, and that person can send you for other help and you don't have to prove your poverty over and over and over again.

I have come out of my despair to tell you this. Remember I did not come from another place or another time. Others like me are all around you. Look at us with an angry heart, anger that will help you help me. Anger that will let you tell of me. The poor are always silent. Can you be silent, too?

圆满的结局

[加拿大] 玛格丽特·阿特伍德

约翰和玛丽邂逅了,
接下来会发生什么?
如果你希望一个圆满的结局,尝试A。

A.

约翰和玛丽相爱,并且结了婚。他们都有一份有价值的、报酬丰厚的工作,不乏刺激和兴趣。他们买了一幢漂亮的房子后,房地产开始升值。最后,当他们雇得起居家保姆时,他们生了两个孩子,并把精力投入到他们身上。孩子成长喜人。约翰和玛丽的夫妻生活有刺激有兴趣,两人也有值得交往的朋友。他们一起度过有趣的假期。然后他们退休了。他们都有自己的爱好,不乏刺激和兴趣。最后,他们终老。这就是故事的结局。

B.

玛丽爱上了约翰,但是约翰不爱玛丽。他仅仅是自私地利用她的身体取乐,以一种温和的方式自我满足。他每周去她的公寓两次,她给他做晚餐，你会发现他甚至觉得她连一顿晚餐都不值。等他吃过晚餐，他和她上床，然后他睡自己的觉，而她则去洗碟子，以免他觉得她不爱干净，把脏碟子放着不洗。她还重新涂上唇膏，等他醒来时自己的样子看上去好看。可是等他醒来，他甚至都没注意到这一点，他依次穿上他的短袜、短裤、裤子、衬衫，戴上他的领带，最后穿上他的鞋子，跟脱掉时的顺序正好相反。他从不给玛丽脱衣服，她自己动手，她每次都表现得如饥似渴。倒不是因为她喜欢性，而是想让约翰以为她喜欢，因为只要他们经常上床，他就会渐渐习惯她，渐渐对她产生依恋，最后他们就会结婚。但是，约翰甚至连一句晚安也没说就开门走了。三天后，他在六点准时出现，然后他们把整个过程再重复一遍。

玛丽崩溃了，哭只会让自己脸色难看。人人都知道，但玛丽就是停不下来，工作的同事都注意到了。她的朋友劝她说约翰是一个卑鄙小人、贪婪的人、无赖，他配不上她，但是她不信。她觉得约翰身体里住着一个更好的约翰，只要给第一个约翰施加足够的压力，好约翰就会像破茧的蝴蝶、魔术箱出来的玩偶、梅干上的坑一样跳出来。

一天晚上，约翰抱怨她做的饭菜，以前他从没有抱怨过，玛丽感到十分受伤。

她的朋友跟她说他们看见他在饭店和另一个女人在一起。那女人叫玛奇。倒不是玛奇伤到了玛丽，是饭店伤了玛丽。约翰从来没有带玛丽去过饭店。玛丽把所有她能够找到的安眠药和阿司匹林用半瓶雪利酒送了下去。她没喝威士忌，你可以就此看出她是一个什么样的女人。她给约翰留了一张纸条。她希望他能及时发现她，然后送她去医院，感到忏悔，然后和她结婚。然而这一切并没有发生，她死了。

约翰娶了玛奇，然后一切像 A 一样继续发展。

C.

约翰,一个老男人,爱上了玛丽;玛丽,年仅二十二岁,同情约翰因为他担心脱发。她因工作结识了他,虽然不爱他却和他上了床。她喜欢的人叫詹姆士,也年仅二十二岁,也是一个没有准备稳定下来的人。

与詹姆士相反,约翰很早就稳定下来,这也是困扰他的地方。约翰有一份稳定、体面的工作,在他所在的领域如日中天。但玛丽对他的印象不深刻,她对詹姆士印象深刻,他拥有一辆摩托车,还收藏了大量唱片。但是,詹姆士经常骑着他的摩托车东奔西跑,自由自在。自由在女孩看来并不一样,所以与此同时,玛丽周四晚上都和约翰在一起,每周四是约翰唯一能抽出身来的时间。

约翰和一个叫玛奇的女人结了婚。他们生了两个孩子,还有一间漂亮的房子,是在房地产刚升值前买的。夫妇俩有很多爱好:只要有时间,他们会使自己的爱好既刺激又有趣。约翰告诉玛丽她对他有多重要,但是他当然不会离开他的妻子,因为婚约就是婚约。约翰继续说着甜言蜜语,玛丽感觉烦透了。不过老男人有办法让时间维持得更长久,所以总的来说,玛丽度过了一段相当不错的时光。

有一天,詹姆士骑着他的顶级加州混合动力摩托车轻快地驶了进来。詹姆士和玛丽比你想象的兴致还要高,他们爬上了床。一切都顺理成章。但是,约翰也随之出现了,他有玛丽公寓的钥匙。他看到他们飘飘欲仙地纠缠在一起。考虑到玛奇,他几乎找不到妒忌的理由。但他仍感到完全绝望了。他人到中年,头会在两年内秃得像鸡蛋一样,他受不了。他买了一把手枪,说是为了打靶练习——这是阴谋的薄弱环节,不过很快得到了弥补——他射向了他们两个,然后朝自己开了枪。

玛奇,度过了一段悲伤的调整期后,嫁给了一个善解人意的人,名叫弗雷德,一切像 A 一样继续发展,只不过换了名字而已。

D.

弗雷德和玛奇之间没什么矛盾，相处得出奇地好，他们擅长解决也许会出现的各种小困难。但是他们漂亮的房子坐落在海边，一天，一个巨浪逼近，房地产随之贬值。余下的故事是关于巨浪的成因以及他们如何逃生。上千人被淹死了，他们却没有，因为他们品德高尚，善于感恩，然后一切如 A 般进行。

E.

一切都没错，不过弗雷德的心脏状况糟糕。余下的是关于弗雷德死前和玛奇多么善良、多么善解人意的故事。然后玛奇投身于慈善事业直到一切像 A 一样结束。如果你喜欢，故事可以叫"玛奇""癌症""内疚与困惑"和"观察野鸟的爱好"。

F.

如果你觉得这些太平庸，那么假设约翰是一个革命者，玛丽是一个反间谍活动调查员，你看他们能走多远。记住，这里是加拿大。即使你得到一个桃色的激情澎湃的长篇英雄故事，有点像我们当代的编年史，你最终还是会像 A 一样结束。

你只能面对事实，不论你怎样删减，结局都毫无二致。不要被其他结局欺骗了，它们都是假的。要么是心怀不轨故意造假，要么假如不是完全的多愁善感，那就是过度乐观导致的。

唯一真实可靠的结局在这里：

约翰和玛丽死了，约翰和玛丽死了，约翰和玛丽死了。

结局够多的了，开头总是更有趣。真正的行家懂得品味故事的弹性部分，这是最奈何不得的部分。

这些是跟情节有关的所有讨论，无论怎样就是一件事情跟着一件事情，一个什么，一个什么，然后一个什么。

　　现在尝试怎么样和为什么吧。

Happy Endings

By Margaret Atwood

John and Mary meet.

What happens next?

If you want a happy ending, try A.

A.

John and Mary fall in love and get married. They both have worthwhile and remunerative jobs which they find stimulating and challenging. They buy a charming house. Real estate values go up. Eventually, when they can afford live-in help, they have two children, to whom they are devoted. The children turn out well. John and Mary have a stimulating and challenging sex life and worthwhile friends. They go on fun vacations together. They retire. They both have hobbies which they find stimulating and challenging. Eventually they die. This is the end of the story.

B.

Mary falls in love with John but John doesn't fall in love with Mary. He merely uses her body for selfish pleasure and ego gratification of a tepid kind. He comes to her apartment twice a week and she cooks him dinner, you'll notice that he doesn't even consider her worth the price of a dinner out, and after he's eaten dinner he fucks her and after that he falls asleep, while she does the dishes so he won't think she's untidy, having all those dirty dishes lying around, and puts on fresh lipstick so she'll look good when he wakes up, but when he wakes up he doesn't even notice, he puts on his socks and his shorts and his pants and his shirt and his tie and his shoes, the reverse order from the one in which he took them off. He doesn't take off Mary's clothes, she takes them off herself, she acts as if she's dying for it every time, not because she likes sex exactly, she doesn't, but she wants John to think she does because if they do it often enough surely he'll get used to her, he'll come to depend on her and they will get married, but John goes out the door with hardly so much as a good-night and three days later he turns up at six o'clock and they do the whole thing over again.

Mary gets run-down. Crying is bad for your face, everyone knows that and so does Mary but she can't stop. People at work notice. Her friends tell her John is a rat, a pig, a dog, he isn't good enough for her, but she can't believe it. Inside John, she thinks, is another John, who is much nicer. This other John will emerge like a butterfly from a cocoon, a Jack from a box, a pit from a prune, if the first John is only squeezed enough.

One evening John complains about the food. He has never complained about her food before. Mary is hurt.

Her friends tell her they've seen him in a restaurant with another woman, whose name is Madge. It's not even Madge that finally gets to Mary: it's the restaurant. John has never taken Mary to a restaurant. Mary collects all the sleeping pills and aspirins she can find, and takes them and a half a bottle of sherry. You can see what kind of a woman she is by the fact that it's not even whiskey. She leaves a note for John. She hopes he'll discover her and get her to the hospital in time and repent and then they can get married, but this fails to happen and she dies.

John marries Madge and everything continues as in A.

C.

John, who is an older man, falls in love with Mary, and Mary, who is only twenty-two, feels sorry for him because he's worried about his hair falling out. She sleeps with him even though she's not in love with him. She met him at work. She's in love with someone called James, who is twenty-two also and not yet ready to settle down.

John on the contrary settled down long ago: this is what is bothering him. John has a steady, respectable job and is getting ahead in his field, but Mary isn't impressed by him, she's impressed by James, who has a motorcycle and a fabulous record collection. But James is often away on his motorcycle, being free. Freedom isn't the same for girls, so in the meantime Mary spends Thursday evenings with John. Thursdays are the only days John can get away.

John is married to a woman called Madge and they have two children, a charming house which they bought just before the real estate values went up, and hobbies which they find stimulating and challenging, when they have the time. John tells Mary how important she is to him, but of course he can't leave his wife because a commitment is a commitment. He goes on about this more than is necessary and Mary finds it boring, but older men can keep it up longer so on the whole she has a fairly good time.

One day James breezes in on his motorcycle with some top-grade California hybrid and James and Mary get higher than you'd believe possible and they climb into bed. Everything becomes very underwater, but along comes John, who has a key to Mary's apartment. He finds them stoned and entwined. He's hardly in any position to be jealous, considering Madge, but nevertheless he's overcome with despair. Finally he's middle-aged, in two years he'll be as bald as an egg and he can't stand it. He purchases a handgun, saying he needs it for target practice—this is the thin part of the plot, but it can be dealt with later—and shoots the two of them and himself.

Madge, after a suitable period of mourning, marries an understanding man called Fred and everything continues as in A, but under different names.

D.

Fred and Madge have no problems. They get along exceptionally well and are good at working out any little difficulties that may arise. But their charming house is by the seashore and one day a giant tidal wave approaches. Real estate values go down. The rest of the story is about what caused the tidal wave and how they escape from it. They do, though thousands drown, but Fred and Madge are virtuous and grateful, and continue as in A.

E.

Yes, but Fred has a bad heart. The rest of the story is about how kind and understanding they both are until Fred dies. Then Madge devotes herself to charity work until the end of A. If you like, it can be "Madge," "cancer," "guilty and confused," and "bird watching."

F.

If you think this is all too bourgeois, make John a revolutionary and Mary a counterespionage agent and see how far that gets you.

Remember, this is Canada. You'll still end up with A, though in between you may get a lustful brawling saga of passionate involvement, a chronicle of our times, sort of.

You'll have to face it, the endings are the same however you slice it. Don't be deluded by any other endings, they're all fake, either deliberately fake, with malicious intent to deceive, or just motivated by excessive optimism if not by downright sentimentality.

The only authentic ending is the one provided here:

John and Mary die. John and Mary die. John and Mary die.

So much for endings. Beginnings are always more fun. True connoisseurs, however, are known to favor the stretch in between, since it's the hardest to do anything with.

That's about all that can be said for plots, which anyway are just one thing after another, a what and a what and a what.

Now try How and Why.

入职介绍

[美国] 丹尼尔·奥罗斯科

那些是办公室，这些是小隔间。我的隔间在那儿，这是你的隔间。这部电话是你的，但是有电话来千万不要接，语音信箱系统会自动回复的。这是语音信箱系统使用手册，不允许接打私人电话。但是，我们考虑到每个人都会有紧急情况，所以你要是必须打紧急电话的话，就先请示你的主管。如果找不到主管的话，就问一下坐在那边的菲利普·斯皮尔斯。他会和坐在那边的克拉丽莎·尼克斯商量的。如果你未经申请就打了紧急电话的话，你可能会被辞退。这些是你的收发箱。收件箱中的所有表单必须按左上角显示的日期登录，并由你在右上角签字，然后分发给分析处理员，其名称在左下角用数字编码。右下角是空白的。这是你的分析处理员的数字代码索引。这是你的表格处理程序手册。

你必须调整你的工作节奏。我是什么意思？我很高兴你这样反问。按照规定，我们每天工作八小时，我们必须按照每个工作日工作八小时的规定来安排时间。假如你的收件箱里有十二个小时的工作时间，那你就必须把这项工作压缩成八个小时来完成。如果你的收件箱里有一个小时的工作时间，那就必须把它扩充到一天八个小时。这个问题问得很好，什么问题都随便问。可你要是问太多的话，可能会让你走人。

那是我们的接待员,她是个临时工,我们这里走接待员的流程。他们辞职的频率高得惊人。对临时工要彬彬有礼,记住他们的名字,偶尔邀请他们吃午饭。但是不要和他们走得太近,因为那样的话在他们离开以后情况只会变得更困难。他们总是离开。你完全可以确信这一点。

男厕所在那边。女厕所在那边。坐在那儿的约翰·拉方丹偶尔会用女厕所。他说自己不是故意的,我们都心知肚明,可是我们都绝口不提。约翰·拉方丹不会造成伤害,他闯入女厕所这种禁地仅仅是一种无害的刺激,是他平淡乏味的生活轨迹上的一点微弱的光点。

坐在你左边隔间里的是罗素·纳什,他爱上了坐在你右边隔间里的阿曼达·皮尔斯。他们下班后坐同一辆公共汽车。对阿曼达·皮尔斯来说,这只是一次无聊的巴士之旅,和罗素·纳什东拉西扯能让这段旅程变得不那么乏味。但对于罗素·纳什来说,这是他一天中最激动人心的时刻,也是他一生中最激动人心的时刻。罗素·纳什体重增加了四十磅,每月都会增重。在公司,他一边啃着薯条和饼干,一边忧伤地偷看阿曼达·皮尔斯的小隔间;在家里,他一面吃着冷比萨和冰激凌,一边看电视上的成人视频。

你右边隔间的阿曼达·皮尔斯,有个六岁的儿子,是自闭症患者,名叫杰米。她的小隔间从上到下都贴满他儿子的蜡笔画,每张画上都有精致的黑黄相间的同心圆和椭圆。她每个星期五换一次。记得要对这些画发表评论。阿曼达·皮尔斯还有个当律师的丈夫。他强迫她接受一系列性游戏,这些让她的痛苦和耻辱不断升级,阿曼达·皮尔斯不情愿地服从着。她每天早上来上班的时候都筋疲力尽,带着新伤,胸部擦伤、腹部瘀伤,大腿后面二度烧伤,这些都让她皱眉蹙额。

但我们其实是不该知道这些的。千万别说出去,说出去你就会走人。

一直忍着罗素·纳什的阿曼达·皮尔斯爱上了阿尔伯特·博什,

他的办公室就在那边。阿尔伯特·博什对阿曼达·皮尔斯的存在只有模糊的印象，他只对坐在那里的埃莉·塔珀感兴趣。讨厌阿尔伯特·博什的埃莉·塔珀愿意为柯蒂斯·兰斯赴汤蹈火。但柯蒂斯·兰斯讨厌埃莉·塔珀。这个世界是不是个滑稽的地方？当然了，不是那种会让人哈哈大笑的滑稽。

阿尼卡·布鲁姆坐在那个小隔间里。去年阿尼卡·布鲁姆和巴里·哈克一起参加审查季度报告的会议时，她的左手开始流血。她整个人陷入恍惚之中，盯着自己的手，然后告诉巴里·哈克他的妻子会在什么时间死去，怎么死去。我们当时都没理会，毕竟她是个新职员。但是没想到巴里·哈克的妻子现在真的死了。所以，除非你想确切地知道你会在什么时候死，怎么死，否则不要和阿尼卡·布鲁姆说话。

科林·希维坐在那边的小隔间里。他也曾经跟你一样是新人。我们警告过他阿尼卡·布鲁姆的事。但是去年圣诞聚餐的时候，他看没人和她说话，为她感到难过。科林·希维给她拿了一杯饮料。从那以后他就再不是他自己了。科林·希维是命中该绝。他无能为力，我们也无力帮他。离科林·希维远点儿。不要把你的任何工作交给他。如果他要求你做什么，告诉他你必须先跟我核实。如果他再次要求，告诉他我还没回复你。

这是消防出口。这层楼有好几个，都做了相应的标记。我们每三个月进行一次楼层疏散评估，每个月进行一次逃生路线测试。每年进行两次消防演习，一年进行一次地震演习。这些不过是预防措施而已。这些事永远不会发生。

根据你提供的信息，我们有个全面的健康计划。任何灾难性疾病和不可预见的悲剧都全覆盖。所有家属也都全覆盖。坐在那边的拉里·巴迪基恩有六个女儿。如果他的任何一个女儿或者她们全部同时死于一种可怕的退化性肌肉疾病或某种罕见的有毒血液疾病，或者在课堂实地考察时被半自动的炮火喷射，或是在她们的双层床上被一些潜入的疯子攻击的话，如果发生上述任何一种情况的话，拉里的女儿们都会得到照顾。拉里·巴迪基恩一毛钱都不用付。他没有什么可担心的。

我们还有充足的假期和病假政策。还有极好的残疾保险计划。我们有稳定和盈利的养老基金。我们有交响乐团的团体折扣，还有在棒球场的固定座位。我们得到了这座桥的通勤票。我们用的是直接存款的方式。我们还都是"好市多"的会员。

这是我们的小厨房。这位是我们的咖啡先生。我们有一个咖啡罐，每个人每周花两美元买咖啡、过滤器、糖和咖啡伴侣。如果你喜欢雀巢咖啡或者加一半的咖啡伴侣的话，有个特殊的咖啡罐，一周三美元。如果你喜欢甜食但是不喜欢糖的话，有个每周一百美元的特殊咖啡罐。我们不做脱咖啡因咖啡。你可以选择你喜欢的任何一个咖啡罐，但是不许碰咖啡先生。

这边是微波炉。你可以用这个加热食物。但是你不能在微波炉里做饭。

我们有一小时的午餐时间。上午还有十五分钟的间歇，下午也有十五分钟的间歇。休息的时候一定要休息。如果你错过，就永远失去了。供你参考，你的间歇是一种特权，而不是权利。如果你滥用间歇政策，我们有权取消你的间歇。而午餐，却是一种权利，而不是特权。如果你滥用午餐政策，我们的手都被束缚住了，只能佯作不知。但我们不喜欢那样。

这是冰箱。你可以把午饭放在里面。坐在那边的巴里·哈克偷冰箱里的吃的。他这种小小的盗窃行为是他发泄悲痛的方式。去年除夕，在和妻子接吻的时候，她的大脑出现了血管破裂。巴里·哈克的妻子当时怀孕两个月,持续昏迷了半年之后死了。对巴里·哈克来说,这是一个悲剧性的损失。从那以后他就不再是他自己了。他的妻子是一个漂亮女人。她也被健康计划全覆盖了。巴里·哈克不用付一毛钱。但他死去的妻子的鬼魂长期不断地缠绕着他,也缠绕着我们所有人。我们见过她,在电脑显示器上反射出来,穿过我们的隔间。我们在影印本上看到过她脸上暗淡的影子。她在接待员的预约簿上用铅笔写着"要见巴里·哈克"。还在语音信箱里留言,电邮发出的刺耳的声音和电话线上的嗡嗡声使留言变得模糊不清,她的声音从很远的地方回响着,与周围的嗡嗡声混在一起。但人声是她的。在这个人声下面,在静电和嘶嘶声的潮水般的哗哗声中,还能听到婴儿咯咯的笑声和哭声。

无论如何,如果你带午餐的话,就在巴里·哈克的包里多放点小东西吧。我们办公室有四个巴里。这不是巧合吗?

这是马修·佩恩的办公室。他是我们的部门经理,他的门总是关着的。我们从来没有见过他,你也永远不会见到他。但是他就在那里,对此你可以肯定。他就在我们左右。

这是管理员的壁橱。管理员的壁橱和你没什么关系。

这是我们的储藏柜。如果你的储备物资用完了的话,就去找柯蒂斯·兰斯。他会把你的需要记在储藏柜授权日志上,然后给你一张物资授权单。给艾丽·川普看下你的粉色供货授权单复制版。她会把你记录在储藏柜钥匙日志上,然后把钥匙给你。因为物资柜在部门经理办公室外面,所以你一定要非常安静,静悄悄地拿你的东西。储藏柜隔成四个格子。第一个格子有信纸、空白纸、信封、记录本和记事本等。第二个格子里有钢笔、铅笔、打字机和打印机色带等。第三个格子里有橡皮擦、修正液、透明胶带、胶棒,等等。第四个格子里有回形针、图钉、剪刀和刀片。这是碎纸机的备用刀片。别碰那里的碎纸机。碎纸机与你无关。

格温多琳·斯蒂奇在那边的那个办公室。她特别喜欢企鹅，收集了很多关于企鹅的小摆设：企鹅海报、咖啡杯和文具、企鹅玩具、企鹅珠宝、企鹅毛衣、T恤和袜子。加班晚了的话她就会穿企鹅毛绒拖鞋。她有一盒企鹅叫声的磁带，她听企鹅的声音是为了放松。她最喜欢的颜色是黑白。她的车牌很有个性，上面写着潘·格温（和企鹅发音相同）。每天早晨，她都要经过所有的小隔间和每个人说早上好。她会在每周三的驼峰日上午休息时带上丹尼斯，周五下午休息时带着甜甜圈。她组织每年的圣诞聚餐，并负责生日清单。格温多琳·斯蒂奇的门总是对我们所有人敞开着。她总是善于倾听，替你说好话；她总是给予我们帮助，或者倾囊相助，提供一个哭泣时所需要的肩膀。因为她的门总是开着的，所以她想哭的时候就躲在女厕所的小隔间里。约翰·拉方丹，当一个女人进来的时候，他被迷住了，静静地坐在他的隔间里，膝盖抵着胸口，约翰·拉方丹听到她在里面呕吐。我们看到格温多琳·斯蒂奇蜷缩在楼梯间，在上升气流中颤抖，啜饮着毕比先生的食物，抱着膝盖。她不让这些干扰她的工作。如果这件事妨碍了她的工作，可能会让她走人。

坐在那边小隔间里的是凯文·霍华德。他是个连环杀手，他们称之为地毯切割工，全城的死伤都与他有关。我们不应该知道这些的，所以你千万别说出去。别担心。他只会对陌生人产生强迫心理，这种固定程序制定得精细，也很难改变。受害者必须是个30岁以下的白人成年男子，身材魁梧，黑头发黑眼睛，诸如此类的要求。在日落前，必须从公共场所随机选择受害者，跟踪受害者回家然后进行一番打斗，等等。谋杀的结果十分精确：切口的角度和方向，皮肤和肌肉组织的分层，内脏器官的重新排列，等等。凯文·霍华德不会让这些事干扰他的工作。事实上，他是我们中间打字速度最快的人。他打字的时候简直像着火了似的。他暗恋格温多琳·斯蒂奇，每天下午都会在她的办公桌上留下一个红色的箔纸包好的好时巧克力。但他很讨厌阿尼卡·布鲁姆，而且离她远远的。他在场的时候，她浑身颤抖，无法控制，左手一直在流血。

谁能想到呢，当凯文·霍华德被抓的时候，他表现得很惊讶。说他看起来像个好人，就是有时候有点孤僻，但总是安安静静、彬彬有礼的。

这里是复印室。这边就是我们平常可以看到的风景。复印室面向西南。西面在那里，朝着水的方向。北面在后面。因为我们在十七楼，所以能看到这么壮观的景色。是不是很美？在这儿可以俯瞰公园，树梢就在那里。你可以看到那边两栋楼之间的一段海湾。你可以看到太阳就在那两栋楼之间的缝隙里落下。你可以看到这座建筑能在对面那座建筑的玻璃板上反射出来。那里。看到了吗？那是你啊，快挥挥手。你再看那里，小厨房里的阿尼卡·布鲁姆正在向你挥手呢。

复印的时候就欣赏这些风景吧。如果复印机有问题，就去见罗素·纳什。如果你有任何问题，就请示你的主管。如果你找不到你的主管，问问坐在那边的菲利普·斯皮尔斯。他会和坐在那个地方的克拉丽莎·尼克斯商量的。如果你找不到他们的话可以随时问我。那边就是我的隔间。我坐在那里。

Orientation

By Daniel Orozco

Those are the offices and these are the cubicles. That's my cubicle there, and this is your cubicle. This is your phone. Never answer your phone. Let the Voicemail System answer it. This is your Voicemail System Manual. There are no personal phone calls allowed. We do, however, allow for emergencies. If you must make an emergency phone call, ask your supervisor first. If you can't find your supervisor, ask Phillip Spiers, who sits over there. He'll check with Clarissa Nicks, who sits over there. If you make an emergency phone call without asking, you may be let go. These are your in- and out-boxes. All the forms in your inbox must be logged in by the date shown in the upper-left-hand corner, initialed by you in the upper-right-hand corner, and distributed to the Processing Analyst whose name is numerically coded in the lower-left-hand corner. The lower-right-hand corner is left blank. Here's your Processing Analyst Numerical Code Index. And here's your Forms Processing Procedures Manual.

You must pace your work. What do I mean? I'm glad you asked that. We pace our work according to the eight-hour workday. If you have twelve hours of work in your in-box, for example, you must compress that work into the eight-hour day. If you have one hour of work in your in-box, you must expand that work to fill the eight-hour day. That was a good question. Feel free to ask questions. Ask too many questions, however, and you may be let go.

That is our receptionist. She is a temp. We go through receptionists here. They quit with alarming frequency. Be polite and civil to the temps. Learn their names, and invite them to lunch occasionally. But don't get close to them, as it only makes it more difficult when they leave. And they always leave. You can be sure of that.

The men's room is over there. The women's room is over there. John LaFountaine, who sits over there, uses the women's room occasionally. He says it is accidental. We know better, but we let it pass. John LaFountaine is harmless, his forays into the forbidden territory of the women's room simply a benign thrill, a faint blip on the dull, flat line of his life.

Russell Nash, who sits in the cubicle to your left, is in love with Amanda Pierce, who sits in the cubicle to your right. They ride the same bus together after work. For Amanda Pierce, it is just a tedious bus ride made less tedious by the idle nattering of

Russell Nash. But for Russell Nash, it is the highlight of his day. It is the highlight of his life. Russell Nash has put on forty pounds and grows fatter with each passing month, nibbling on chips and cookies while peeking glumly over the partitions at Amanda Pierce and gorging himself at home on cold pizza and ice cream while watching adult videos on TV.

Amanda Pierce, in the cubicle to your right, has a six-year old son named Jamie, who is autistic. Her cubicle is plastered from top to bottom with the boy's crayon artwork—sheet after sheet of precisely drawn concentric circles and ellipses, in black and yellow. She rotates them every other Friday. Be sure to comment on them. Amanda Pierce also has a husband, who is a lawyer. He subjects her to an escalating array of painful and humiliating sex games, to which Amanda Pierce reluctantly submits. She comes to work exhausted and freshly wounded each morning, wincing from the abrasions on her breasts, or the bruises on her abdomen, or the second-degree burns on the backs of her thighs.

But we're not supposed to know any of this. Do not let on. If you let on, you may be let go.

Amanda Pierce, who tolerates Russell Nash, is in love with Albert Bosch, whose office is over there. Albert Bosch, who only dimly registers Amanda Pierce's existence, has eyes only for Ellie Tapper, who sits over there. Ellie Tapper, who hates Albert Bosch, would walk through fire for Curtis Lance. But Curtis Lance hates

Ellie Tapper. Isn't the world a funny place? Not in the ha-ha sense, of course.

Anika Bloom sits in that cubicle. Last year, while reviewing quarterly reports in a meeting with Barry Hacker, Anika Bloom's left palm began to bleed. She fell into a trance, stared into her hand, and told Barry Hacker when and how his wife would die. We laughed it off. She was, after all, a new employee. But Barry Hacker's wife is dead. So unless you want to know exactly when and how you'll die, never talk to Anika Bloom.

Colin Heavey sits in that cubicle over there. He was new once, just like you. We warned him about Anika Bloom. But at last year's Christmas Potluck he felt sorry for her when he saw that no one was talking to her. Colin Heavey brought her a drink. He hasn't been himself since. Colin Heavey is doomed. There's nothing he can do about it, and we are powerless to help him. Stay away from Colin Heavey. Never give any of your work to him. If he asks to do something, tell him you have to check with me. If he asks again, tell him I haven't gotten back to you.

This is the fire exit. There are several on this floor, and they are marked accordingly. We have a Floor Evacuation Review every three months, and an Escape Route Quiz once a month. We have our Biannual Fire Drill twice a year, and our Annual Earthquake Drill once a year. These are precautions only. These things never happen.

For your information, we have a comprehensive health plan. Any catastrophic illness, any unforeseen tragedy, is completely covered. All dependents are completely covered. Larry Bagdikian, who sits over there, has six daughters. If anything were to happen to any of his girls, or to all of them, if all six were to simultaneously fall victim to illness or injury—stricken with a hideous degenerative muscle disease or some rare toxic blood disorder, sprayed with semiautomatic gunfire while on a class field trip, or attacked in their bunk beds by some prowling nocturnal lunatic—if any of this were to pass, Larry's girls would all be taken care of. Larry Bagdikian would not have to pay one dime. He would have nothing to worry about.

We also have a generous vacation and sick leave policy. We have an excellent disability insurance plan. We have a stable and profitable pension fund. We get group discounts for the symphony, and block seating at the ballpark. We get commuter ticket books for the bridge. We have direct deposit. We are all members of Costco.

This is our kitchenette. And this, this is our Mr. Coffee. We have a coffee pool into which we each pay two dollars a week for coffee, filters, sugar, and Coffee-mate. If you prefer Cremora or half-and-half to Coffee-mate, there is a special pool for three dollars a week. If you prefer "Sweet'N Low" to sugar, there is a special pool for two-fifty a week. We do not do decaf. You are allowed to join the coffee pool of your choice, but you are not allowed to touch the Mr. Coffee.

This is the micro wave oven. You are allowed to heat food in the microwave oven. You are not, however, allowed to cook food in the microwave oven.

We get one hour for lunch. We also get one fifteen-minute break in the morning and one fifteen-minute break in the afternoon. Always take your breaks. If you skip a break, it is gone forever. For your information, your break is a privilege, not a right. If you abuse the break policy, we are authorized to rescind your breaks. Lunch, however, is a right, not a privilege. If you abuse the lunch policy, our hands will be tied and we will be forced to look the other way. We will not enjoy that.

This is the refrigerator. You may put your lunch in it. Barry Hacker, who sits over there, steals food from this refrigerator. His petty theft is an outlet for his grief. Last New Year's Eve, while kissing his wife, a blood vessel burst in her brain. Barry Hacker's wife was two months pregnant at the time and lingered in a coma for half a year before she died. It was a tragic loss for Barry Hacker. He hasn't been himself since. Barry Hacker's wife was a beautiful woman. She was also completely covered. Barry Hacker did not have to pay one dime. But his dead wife haunts him. She haunts all of us. We have seen her, reflected in the monitors of our computers, moving past our cubicles. We have seen the dim shadow of her face in our photocopies. She pencils herself in the receptionist's appointment book with the notation "To see Barry Hacker." She has left messages in the receptionist's Voicemail box, messages garbled by the electronic chirrups and buzzes in the phone line, her voice echoing from an immense distance within the ambient hum. But the voice is hers. And beneath the voice, beneath the tidal whoosh of static and hiss, the gurgling and crying of a baby can be heard.

In any case, if you bring a lunch, put a little something extra in the bag for Barry Hacker. We have four Barrys in this office. Isn't that a coincidence?

This is Matthew Payne's office. He is our Unit Manager, and his door is always closed. We have never seen him, and you will never see him. But he is there. You can be sure of that. He is all around us.

This is the Custodian's Closet. You have no business in the Custodian's Closet.

And this, this is our Supplies Cabinet. If you need supplies, see Curtis Lance. He will log you in on the Supplies Cabinet Authorization Log, then give you a Supplies Authorization Slip. Present your pink copy of the Supplies Authorization Slip to Ellie Tapper. She will log you in on the Supplies Cabinet Key Log, then give you the key. Because the Supplies Cabinet is located outside the Unit Manager's office, you must be very quiet. Gather your supplies quietly. The Supplies Cabinet is divided into four sections. Section One contains letterhead stationery, blank paper and envelopes, memo pads and note pads, and so on. Section Two contains pens and pencils and typewriter and printer ribbons, and the like. In Section Three we have erasers, correction fluids, transparent tapes, glue sticks, et cetera. And in Section Four we have paper clips and pushpins and scissors and razor blades. And here are the spare blades for the shredder. Do not touch the shredder, which is located over there. The shredder is of no concern to you.

Gwendolyn Stich sits in that office there. She is crazy about penguins and collects penguin knickknacks: penguin posters and coffee mugs and stationery, penguin stuffed animals, penguin jewelry, penguin sweaters and T-shirts and socks. She has a pair of penguin fuzzy slippers she wears when working late at the office. She has a tape cassette of penguin sounds, which she listens to for relaxation. Her favorite colors are black and white. She has personalized license plates that read PEN GWEN. Every morning, she passes through all the cubicles to wish each of us a *good* morning. She brings Danish on Wednesdays for Hump Day morning break, and doughnuts on Fridays for TGIF afternoon break. She organizes the Annual Christmas Potluck and is in charge of the Birthday List. Gwendolyn Stich's door is always open to all of us. She will always lend an ear and put in a good word for you; she will always give you a hand, or the shirt off her back, or a shoulder to cry on. Because her door is always open, she hides and cries in a stall in the women's room. And John LaFountaine—who, enthralled when a woman enters, sits quietly in his stall with his knees to his chest—John LaFountaine has heard her vomiting in there. We have come upon Gwendolyn Stich huddled in the stairwell, shivering in the updraft, sipping a Diet Mr. Pibb and hugging her knees. She does not let any of this interfere with her work. If it interfered with her work, she might have to be let go.

Kevin Howard sits in that cubicle over there. He is a serial killer, the one they call the Carpet Cutter, responsible for the mutilations across town. We're not supposed to know that, so do not let on. Don't worry. His compulsion inflicts itself on strangers only, and the routine established is elaborate and unwavering. The victim must be a white male, a young adult no older than thirty, heavyset, with dark hair and eyes, and the like. The victim must be chosen at random before sunset, from a public place; the victim is followed home and must put up a struggle; et cetera. The carnage inflicted is precise: the angle and direction of the incisions, the layering of skin and muscle tissue, the rearrangement of visceral organs, and so on. Kevin Howard does not let any of this interfere with his work. He is, in fact, our fastest typist. He types as if he were on fire. He has a secret crush on Gwendolyn Stich and leaves a red-foil-wrapped Hershey's Kiss on her desk every afternoon. But he hates Anika Bloom and keeps well away from her. In his presence, she has uncontrollable fits of shaking and trembling. Her left palm does not stop bleeding.

In any case, when Kevin Howard gets caught, act surprised. Say that he seemed like a nice person, a bit of a loner, perhaps, but always quiet and polite.

This is the photocopier room. And this, this is our view. It faces southwest. West is down there, toward the water. North is back there. Because we are on the seventeenth floor, we are afforded a magnificent view. Isn't it beautiful? It overlooks the park, where the tops of those trees are. You can see a segment of the bay between those two buildings over there. You can see the sun set in the gap between those two buildings over there. You can see this building reflected in the glass panels of that building across the way. There. See? That's you, waving. And look there. There's Anika Bloom in the kitchenette, waving back.

Enjoy this view while photocopying. If you have problems with the photocopier, see Russell Nash. If you have any questions, ask your supervisor. If you can't find your supervisor, ask Phillip Spiers. He sits over there. He'll check with Clarissa Nicks. She sits over there. If you can't find them, feel free to ask me. That's my cubicle. I sit in there.

2053年的夜行人

[美国] 雷·布拉德伯里

十一月的一个晚上八点,出得门来,进入笼罩在白雾茫茫中的寂静的城市,双脚踩在粗糙的混凝土人行道上,跨过长满草的地砖缝隙,双手插在口袋里,穿过一片寂静,向前进,这是伦纳德·米德先生最喜欢做的事。此时是公元2053年,他独自一人在这个世界上,或者说相当于独自一人。他已经做出了最终决定,选择了一条路,他会大踏步地向前进,呼出的冰冷的哈气像雪茄的烟雾。

这是十一月初的一个晚上。空气中到处弥漫着冰霜。冰霜割在鼻子上,胸中却暗藏火焰,就好像胸中有一棵圣诞树,树枝上挂满了看不见的白雪,但你却可以感受到外面忽明忽暗的寒光。他聆听着自己柔软的鞋底踩在秋天的落叶上发出的轻轻的脚步声,感到心满意足。口哨声从他的齿间传出,声音宁静而清冽。他边走边偶尔捡起一片落叶,在不易遇到的灯光下观察它的骨架图案,嗅着它散发出的腐烂气味。

这条长街静悄悄的,空无一人,只有他的身影在移动,仿佛乡野上空翱翔的一只雄鹰。如果他闭上眼睛,停下脚步,纹丝不动,他的脑海中就会浮现出自己站在平坦、寒冷、无风的亚利桑那沙漠中心,方圆一千英里之内没有任何房舍,陪伴他的只有干涸的河床和街道。在这十年里,他走过了数千英里,不论是白昼还是黑夜,却从未遇到任何一个行人,一个也没有。

他转身走进了一条小街,沿着蜿蜒的小路朝他家走去。在距他家只有一个街区的时候,突然一辆汽车一个急转弯出现在他面前,他身上闪过一道强烈的白色光锥。他如醉如痴地站着,就像一只夜蛾,被光照得目瞪口呆,然后向它走去。过了一小会儿,他缓过神来,朝那辆车走去。

一个金属似的声音向他喊话:"站在那里!原地别动!不许动!"他停了脚步。"举起手来!""可是……"他说。"举起手来!否则,我们就开枪啦!"当然,这是警车,尽管见到警车是一件非常罕见且令人难以置信的事情。在这座拥有 300 万人口的城市,只剩下了一辆警车,难道这不对吗?从一年前,也就是 2052 大选年开始,警方就已经把警车从原来的三辆削减到了一辆。犯罪率持续降低,已经不需要警察了,留下这辆孤零零的警车在空空荡荡的街道上闲来荡去。

"你叫什么名字?"警车上传出金属似的低声问讯。强光刺眼,他看不到警车上的人。"伦纳德·米德。"他回答道。"大声回答!""伦纳德·米德!""经商还是职业?""我想你可以称我为作家。""无业。"警车说道,好像在自言自语。光线像针一样刺透他的胸,把他固定在那里,看起来仿佛博物馆中的一件标本。

"你可以这么说吧。"米德先生说。他已经多年没写过东西了,现在也不卖杂志和书籍。"无业。"留声机似的声音再次响起,同时夹杂着嘶嘶声。"你出来干什么?""走走。"伦纳德·米德回答说。"走走!""对,只是走走。"他简单地回答,但表情有些冷漠。"走走,只是走走,走走?""是的,警官。""往哪里走?为什么要走?""出来走走看看,透透气。"

"你的地址！""圣詹姆斯南街11号。""你家里有空气，也有空调，是吧，米德先生？""有。""你家里也装了观景屏？""没有。""没有？"然后，从寂静中传出一阵噼里啪啦的声音，应该是警方在记录控诉理由。"你结婚了吗，米德先生？""没有。"

"未婚。"强光束后传来警察的声音。此时此刻，明月高挂，繁星点点，煞是可爱。一幢幢房屋灰蒙蒙的，静静矗立。"没人要我。"伦纳德·米德微笑着说。"问你再说话！"伦纳德·米德在寒夜中等待着。"只是走走，米德先生？""是的。""可是，你还没有解释走的目的。"

"我已经解释过了，出来看看透透气，只是走走嘛。""你经常这样做吗？""每天晚上都会出来走走，好多年了。"警车停靠在街道中央，车上的收音机里发出轻轻的嗡嗡声。"好的，米德先生。"警车中的声音说道。"完了？"他彬彬有礼地问道。"完了。"那个声音回答道。"进来。"此时传来一声叹息和砰的一声，警车的后排车门弹开了。"上车。"

"等一下，我什么也没干呀！""上车。""我抗议！""米德先生，请你上车。"突然间，他的走路姿势变得像一个醉汉。当他经过汽车前车窗时，他向里面看了一眼。正如他所料，前排座位上并没有人，车里一个人也没有。"上车。"

他将手放在车门上，凝视着后座。后排座椅其实是一个小囚室，一个带有栏杆的黑色小囚室。囚室里散发着铆接钢的味道，还有浓浓的防腐剂的味道。它闻起来过于干净、过于生硬，带着浓重的金属味。那里的东西没一样是软的。

"如果你有妻子，她还能帮你提供不在场证明，"那个铁一样的声音说道，"但是……""你们要带我去哪儿？""去'精神病患者回归社会趋向研究中心'。"他上了车。车门轻轻地关上了。警车前面闪烁着微弱的灯,穿过黑夜中的林荫大道。

片刻过后,他们经过一条街上的一幢房屋旁,城内所有的房屋都是漆黑一片,只有这幢特别的房屋灯火通明。每个正方形的窗口都发出明亮、黄色的光,在清冷的夜色中很是温暖。"那栋房子是我家。"伦纳德·米德说。但没有人答话。

The Pedestrian

By Ray Bradbury

To enter out into that silence that was the city at eight o'clock of a misty evening in November, to put your feet upon that buckling concrete walk, to step over grassy seams and make your way, hands in pockets, through the silences, that was what Mr. Leonard Mead most dearly loved to do. He was alone in this world of 2053 A.D., or as good as alone, and with a final decision made, a path selected, he would stride off, sending patterns of frosty air before him like the smoke of a cigar.

It was an early November evening. There was a good crystal frost in the air; it cut the nose and made the lungs blaze like a Christmas tree inside; you could feel the cold light going on and off, all the branches filled with invisible snow. He listened to the faint push of his soft shoes through autumn leaves with satisfaction, and whistled a cold quiet whistle between his teeth, occasionally picking up a leaf as he passed, examining its skeletal pattern in the infrequent lamplights as he went on, smelling its rusty smell.

The street was silent and long and empty, with only his shadow moving like the shadow of a hawk in mid-country. If he closed his eyes and stood very still, frozen, he could imagine himself upon the centre of a plain, a wintry, windless Arizona desert with no house in a thousand miles, and only dry river beds, the street, for company. In ten years of walking by night or day, for thousands of miles, he had never met another person walking, not one in all that time.

He turned back on a side street, circling around toward his home. He was within a block of his destination when the lone car turned a corner quite suddenly and flashed a fierce white cone of light upon him. He stood entranced, not unlike a night moth, stunned by the illumination, and then drawn toward it.

A metallic voice called to him: "Stand still. Stay where you are! Don't move!" He halted. "Put up your hands!" "But-" he said. "Your hands up! Or we'll shoot!" The police, of course, but what a rare, incredible thing; in a city of three million, there was only one police car left, wasn't that correct? Ever since a year ago, 2052, the election year, the force had been cut down from three cars to one. Crime was ebbing; there was no need now for the police, save for this one lone car wandering and wandering the empty streets.

"Your name?" said the police car in a metallic whisper. He couldn't see the men in it for the bright light in his eyes. "Leonard

Mead," he said. "Speak up!" "Leonard Mead!" "Business or profession?" "I guess you'd call me a writer." "No profession," said the police car, as if talking to itself. The light held him fixed, like a museum specimen, needle thrust through chest.

"You might say that," said Mr.Mead. He hadn't written in years. Magazines and books didn't sell anymore. "No profession," said the phonograph voice, hissing. "What are you doing out?" "Walking." said Leonard Mead. "Walking!" "Just walking." he said simply, but his face felt cold. "Walking, just walking, walking?" "Yes, sir." "Walking where? For what?"

"Walking for air. Walking to see."

"Your address!" "Eleven South Saint James Street."

"And there is air in your house, you have an air conditioner, Mr. Mead?" "Yes." "And you have a viewing screen in your house to see with?" "No." "No?" There was a crackling quiet that in itself was an accusation. "Are you married, Mr. Mead?" "No."

"Not married," said the police voice behind the fiery beam. The moon was high and dear among the stars and the houses were gray and silent. "Nobody wanted me," said Leonard Mead with a smile. "Don't speak unless you're spoken to!" Leonard Mead waited in the cold night. "Just walking, Mr. Mead?" "Yes." "But you haven't explained for what purpose."

"I explained; for air, and to see, and just to walk." "Have

you done this often?" "Every night for years." The police car sat in the centre of the street with its radio throat faintly humming. "Well, Mr. Mead," it said. "Is that all?" he asked politely. "Yes," said the voice. "Here." There was a sigh, a pop. The back door of the police car sprang wide. "Get in."

"Wait a minute, I haven't done anything!" "Get in." "I protest!" "Mr. Mead." He walked like a man suddenly drunk. As he passed the front window of the car he looked in. As he had expected, there was no one in the front seat, no one in the car at all. "Get in."

He put his hand to the door and peered into the back seat, which was a little cell, a little black jail with bars. It smelled of riveted steel. It smelled of harsh antiseptic; it smelled too clean and hard and metallic. There was nothing soft there.

"Now if you had a wife to give you an alibi," said the iron voice. "But-" "Where are you taking me?" "To the Psychiatric Centre for Research on Regressive Tendencies." He got in. The door shut with a soft thud. The police car rolled through the night avenues, flashing its dim lights ahead.

They passed one house on one street a moment later, one house in an entire city of houses that were dark, but this one particular house had all of its electric lights brightly lit, every window a loud yellow illumination, square and warm in the cool darkness. "That's my house," said Leonard Mead. No one answered him.

身体最重要的部位

从前,我母亲经常问我,身体最重要的部位是什么。许多年来,我一直以为自己所想的是正确答案。

当我很小的时候,我认为对于我们人类来说,声音很重要,所以我回答:"妈咪,我的耳朵最重要。"

她却说道:"不对,有许多人是聋人。但是你继续思考,回头我会再问你。"

几年以后,她又问我。自从第一次回答以后,我就一直苦思冥想正确答案。所以这次我对她说:"妈咪,视觉对每个人都很重要,所以答案应该是我们的眼睛。"

她看着我,对我说:"你学习进步很快,不过答案还是不对,因为有许多人是盲人啊。"

在接下来的那些年里,她又问了我几次,可是她总是回答:"不对,可是我的孩子,你一年比一年聪明啦。"

去年我祖父去世,大家都很伤心,大家都哭了。轮到我们向祖父做最后的告别时,妈妈看着我,问我:"宝贝,你知道身体最重要的部位是什么了吗?"

她在这种时候问我这个问题,让我非常震惊。我一直以为这只是我和她之间的游戏。她看我一脸迷惑的样子,告诉我:"这个问题很重要,它是你真正开始生活的标志。"我看她热泪盈眶,她说道:"宝贝,最重要的部位是你的肩膀。"

我问道:"是因为它能支撑头吗?"

她回答道:"不是,是因为我们的朋友、我们所爱的人哭泣的时候,它可以提供依靠。宝贝,每个人在一生中都会有需要一个可以依靠着哭泣的肩膀的时候。我只是希望当你需要时,会有爱人和朋友给你一个可以依靠着哭泣的肩膀。"

我当时就顿悟了,原来身体最重要的部位不是利己的,而是对别人的痛苦能感同身受的部位。

What Is the Most Important Part of the Body

My mother used to ask me what the most important part of the body is. Through the years I would guess at what I thought was the correct answer.

When I was younger, I thought sound was very important to us as humans, so I said, "My ears, Mommy."

She said, "No. Many people are deaf. But you keep thinking about it and I will ask you again soon."

Several years passed before she asked me again. Since making my first attempt, I had contemplated the correct answer. So this time I told her, "Mommy, sight is very important to everybody, so it must be our eyes."

She looked at me and told me, "You are learning fast, but the answer is not correct because there are many people who are blind."

Over the years, Mother asked me a couple more times and always her answer was, "No, but you are getting smarter every year, my child."

Then last year, my Grandpa died. Everybody was hurt. Everybody was crying. My mom looked at me when it was our turn to say our final good-bye to Grandpa. She asked me, "Do you know the most important body part yet, my dear?"

I was shocked when she asked me this now. I always thought this was a game between her and me. She saw the confusion on my face and told me, "This question is very important. It shows that you have really lived your life." I saw her eyes well up with tears. She said, "My dear, the most important body part is your shoulder."

I asked, "Is it because it holds up your head?"

She replied, "No, it is because it can hold the head of a friend or loved one when they cry. Everybody needs a shoulder to cry on sometimes in life, my dear. I only hope that you have enough love and friends that you will have a shoulder to cry on when you need it."

Then and there I knew the most important body part is not a selfish one. It is sympathetic to the pain of others.

诚实的乞丐

[阿根廷]费尔南多·索伦蒂诺

他是一个诚实的乞丐。

一天他敲开了一座豪宅的大门。里面的男管家出来问道:"你好,先生。你想要什么,我的好人?"

乞丐回答道:"看在上帝的分儿上,就请你发点善心吧。"

"我得向女主人禀报这件事。"

女主人非常吝啬,听了男管家的禀报后说道:"耶利米,给那个好人一块面包吧。只给一块。而且,如果有的话,就给他一块昨天的。"

耶利米与女主人暗地里相爱,为了讨意中人欢心,选了一块硬得像岩石一样的旧面包,然后把它递给了乞丐。

"给你,我的好人。"他说道,然后就不再称乞丐为先生了。

"上帝会保佑你。"乞丐回答道。

耶利米关上了那扇厚重的栎木大门。乞丐把面包夹在腋下走了。他来到了自己度过无数个日日夜夜的空地上,在一片树荫下坐了下来,开始吃他的面包。突然,他咬到了一个坚硬的东西,感觉一颗臼齿都被咬碎了。可是当他看到从地上捡起的臼齿碎片里还有一枚镶着珍珠和钻石的纯金戒指时,他大吃一惊。

"好幸运啊!"他心想。"如果我把它卖了,这样我就有很多钱了,可以用很长时间。"

但他的诚实随即提出了抗议。"不,不行,"他又想,"我得找到戒指的主人,把它物归原主。"

根据刻在戒指上的两个首字母J.X.,既不笨也不懒的乞丐来到了一家商店,要了一本电话簿,结果发现整个镇上只有艾科索凡娜(Xofaina)一家的姓氏是以X为首的。

感到可以将他的诚实品质付诸实践,乞丐内心充满了快乐。他马上出发去寻找艾科索凡娜家。当他看到那座大房子的时候又大吃一惊,就像他看到那个面包里的戒指一样吃惊。他敲开了大门。

耶利米出现了,问道:"你想要什么,我的好人?"

"在你刚才发善心给我的那块面包里我发现了这枚戒指。"乞丐说。

耶利米接过了戒指,说道:"我得向女主人禀报这件事。"

听了男管家的禀报,女主人高兴得竟然唱起了歌,她惊叹道:"我可真走运啊!上星期揉面做面包时弄丢的戒指现在又失而复得啦!看!这两个字母J.X.,代表的正是我的名字约瑟米娜•艾科索凡娜(Josermina Xofaina)的首字母呀。"

她想了一会儿,又补充说:"耶利米,去,看看那位好人想要什么作为回报。只要不太贵,什么都可以。"

耶利米回到了门口,对乞丐说:"我的好人,告诉我你想要什么作为善行的回报呢?"

乞丐回答说:"给我一块能填饱肚子的面包就好。"

耶利米仍然爱着他的女主人,为了讨她的欢心,他找了一块硬得像岩石一样的旧面包,把它递给了乞丐。

"给你,我的好人。"

"上帝会保佑你。"

耶利米关上了那扇厚重的栎木大门。乞丐把面包夹在腋下走了。他来到了自己度过无数个日日夜夜的空地上,在一片树荫下坐了下来,开始吃那块面包。突然,他咬到了一个坚硬的东西,感觉又一颗臼齿被咬碎了。可是当他看到从地上捡起的第二颗臼齿碎片里又有一枚镶着珍珠和钻石的纯金戒指时,又大吃一惊。

又一次,他看到戒指上的那两个首字母J.X.;又一次,他把戒指还给了约瑟米娜·艾科索凡娜;又一次,作为回报,他得到了第三块坚硬的面包;又一次,他发现里面的第三枚戒指,他还了戒指之后,作为回报,他又一次得到了第四块坚硬的面包,里面……

从那个幸运日子开始,一直到他死去的不幸日子,乞丐一直过着快乐的日子,没有经济问题。每天,他只要去还在面包里发现的戒指就行了。

An Honest Beggar

By Fernando Sorrentino

This was a very honest beggar.

One day he knocked at the door of a luxurious mansion. The butler came out and said, "Yes, sir. What do you wish, my good man?"

The beggar answered, "Just a bit of charity, for the love of God."

"I shall have to take this up with the lady of the house."

The butler consulted with the lady of the house and she, who was very miserly, answered. "Jeremiah, give that good man a loaf of bread. One only. And, if possible, one from yesterday."

Jeremiah, who was secretly in love with his employer, in order to please her sought out a stale loaf of bread, hard as a rock, and handed it to the beggar.

"Here you are, my good man." he said, no longer calling him sir.

"God bless you." the beggar answered.

Jeremiah closed the massive oaken door, and the beggar went off with the loaf of bread under his arm. He came to the vacant lot where he spent his days and nights. He sat down in the shade of a tree, and began to eat the bread. Suddenly he bit into a hard object and felt one of his molars crumble to pieces. Great was his surprise when he picked up, together with the fragments of his molar, a fine ring of gold, pearls and diamonds.

"What luck," he said to himself. "I'll sell it and I'll have money for a long time."

But his honesty immediately prevailed. "No," he added. "I'll seek out its owner and return it."

Inside the ring were engraved the initials J. X. Neither unintelligent nor lazy, the beggar went to a store and asked for the telephone book. He found that in the entire town there existed only one family whose surname began with X: the Xofaina family.

Filled with joy for being able to put his honesty into practice, he set out for the home of the Xofaina family. Great was his amazement when he saw it was the very house at which he had been given the loaf of bread containing the ring. He knocked at the door.

Jeremiah emerged and asked him, "What do you wish, my good man?"

The beggar answered, "I've found this ring inside the loaf of bread you were good enough to give me a while ago."

Jeremiah took the ring and said, "I shall have to take this up with the lady of the house."

He consulted with the lady of the house, and she, happy and fairly singing, exclaimed, "Lucky me! Here we are with the ring I had lost last week, while I was kneading the dough for the bread! These are my initials, J.X., which stand for my name: Josermina Xofaina."

After a moment of reflection, she added, "Jeremiah, go and give that good man whatever he wants as a reward. As long as it's not very expensive."

Jeremiah returned to the door and said to the beggar, "My good man, tell me what you would like as a reward for your kind act."

The beggar answered, "Just a loaf of bread to satisfy my hunger."

Jeremiah, who was still in love with his employer, in order to please her sought out an old loaf of bread, hard as a rock, and handed it to the beggar.

"Here you are, my good man."

"God bless you."

Jeremiah shut the massive oaken door, and the beggar went off with the loaf of bread under his arm. He came to the vacant lot in which he spent his days and nights. He sat down in the shade of a tree and began to eat the bread. Suddenly he bit into a hard object and felt another of his molars crumble to pieces. Great was his surprise when he picked up, along with the fragments of this his second broken molar, another fine ring of gold, pearls and diamonds.

Once more he noticed the initials J.X. Once more he returned the ring to Josermina Xofaina and as a reward received a third loaf of hard bread, in which he found a third ring that he again returned and for which lie obtained, as a reward, a fourth loaf of hard bread, in which...

From that fortunate day until the unlucky day of his death, the beggar lived happily and without financial problems. He only had to return the ring he found inside the bread every day.

机智的女儿

在很久很久以前,意大利的一座小镇上有一位商人,他不善经营,欠了一屁股债。债主又老又丑,却对商人貌美的女儿垂涎三尺。于是,他提出要跟商人做笔交易。债主说,只要商人把女儿嫁给他,这笔债就可以一笔勾销。商人和他的女儿一听,顿时惊恐万分。

债主放出话,说他会在一个空袋子里面放一枚黑卵石和一枚白卵石。商人的女儿必须从袋子里面取一枚卵石。如果取出的是黑卵石,就要嫁给他,而她父亲的债也可以一笔勾销;如果取出的是白卵石,就可以不嫁他,而她父亲的债也可以不还了。但如果她拒绝从袋子里面取卵石,债主会让她父亲去坐牢。

他们来到商人家,走在花园的一条铺满卵石的小路上。债主一边跟他们说话,一边捡起两枚卵石。在他俯身捡卵石的时候,女儿眼尖,注意到他捡了两枚黑卵石放进袋中。之后,债主便要商人的女儿从袋子里面取出一枚卵石。

假如你是这个女孩,你会怎么办?如果你可以给她一些建议,你会说什么?仔细分析一下,你会发现这个故事可能会有三种结局:

1. 女孩拒绝从袋中取出卵石。
2. 女孩证明袋中的两枚卵石都是黑的,从而拆穿债主的骗局。
3. 为了替父亲还债,也为了不让父亲坐牢,女孩牺牲自己,从袋中取出一枚黑卵石。

女孩看都没看，就把手伸进袋子，取出了一枚卵石，接着假装手一滑，把卵石掉到了铺满卵石的小路上，这枚卵石便立刻混杂在其他卵石之中，再难寻觅。

"哎呀，看我怎么这么笨手笨脚的。"女儿说。"不过没关系，你只要看看袋里剩下的那枚卵石是什么颜色，就会知道我取出的是黑的还是白的。如果袋子里剩下的卵石是黑色的，那么我取出的肯定是白的。"债主不敢承认自己使出的奸诈手段。于是，商人的女儿成功地将必败的局面扭转成了胜局。

Thinking Out of the Box

Many hundreds of years ago in a small Italian town, a merchant had the misfortune of owing a large sum of money to the moneylender. The moneylender, who was old and ugly, fancied the merchant's beautiful daughter so he proposed a bargain. He said he would forgo the merchant's debt if he could marry the daughter. Both the merchant and his daughter were horrified by the proposal.

The moneylender told them that he would put a black pebble and a white pebble into an empty bag. The girl would then have to pick one pebble from the bag. If she picked the black pebble, she would become the moneylender's wife and her father's debt would be forgiven. If she picked the white pebble she need not marry him and her father's debt would still be forgiven. But if she refused to pick a pebble, her father would be thrown into jail.

They were standing on a pebble strewn path in the merchant's garden. As they talked, the moneylender bent over to pick up two pebbles. As he picked them up, the sharp-eyed girl noticed that he had picked up two black pebbles and put them into the bag. He then asked the girl to pick her pebble from the bag.

What would you have done if you were the girl? If you had to advise her, what would you have told her? Careful analysis would produce three possibilities:

1. The girl should refuse to take a pebble.

2. The girl should show that there were two black pebbles in the bag and expose the moneylender as a cheat.

3. The girl should pick a black pebble and sacrifice herself in order to save her father from his debt and imprisonment.

The girl put her hand into the moneybag and drew out a pebble. Without looking at it, she fumbled and let it fall onto the pebble-strewn path where it immediately became lost among all the other pebbles.

"Oh, how clumsy of me," she said. "But never mind, if you look into the bag for the one that is left, you will be able to tell which pebble I picked. If the remaining pebble is black, it must be assumed that I had picked the white one." The moneylender dared not admit his dishonesty, the girl managed to change what seemed an impossible situation into an advantageous one.

红蚂蚁大战黑蚂蚁

[美国] 亨利·戴维·梭罗

有一天，我出门到我的木材堆去，更确切地说，是树根堆。我看见了两只大蚂蚁在争斗，一只是红的，另一只是黑的，比红的大许多，差不多有半英寸那么长。双方一交手，就谁也不肯放松，搏斗着，扭打着，在木片上不停地滚来滚去。再向远处看去，我惊叹不已，木材堆上这样厮杀的勇士四处可见，看来不是"单挑"，而是"群殴"，是一场发生在两个蚂蚁族群之间的战争。红蚂蚁总是挑战黑蚂蚁，通常是两只红蚂蚁对一只黑蚂蚁。我的堆木场上所有的斜坡和山谷上四处可见这些能征善战的迈密登军团，地上躺满已死的和快死的蚂蚁，有红蚂蚁，也有黑蚂蚁。这是我亲眼所见的唯一一场战役，是我第一次踏上正在酣战中的战地。这一场两败俱伤的生死对决，一方是红色的共和党，一方是黑色的保皇派。双方都在进行殊死搏斗，尽管耳畔不闻嘶吼。我从来没有看到人类的士兵这样奋不顾身。

在一片阳光灿烂的木片小山谷里，一对蚂蚁死死地抱住了对方，此时正值正午，艳阳高照，它们准备战斗到日落，或者战斗到生命的最后一刻。那精瘦的红色勇士像老虎钳一样紧紧咬住死敌的额头不放。双方在战场上滚来滚去，红色勇士在咬断对方的一根触须以后，又咬定了对手另一根触须的根部，一刻也不肯放松。而更强壮的黑蚂蚁则把对手甩过来甩过去。我凑近了看个仔细，发现红蚂蚁的身体有几个部位已经被黑蚂蚁扯掉了。它们比斗牛犬斗得还要顽强。双方都没有一丝一毫的退却表现，显然他们的战争口号是"不成功便成仁"。

　　在小山谷的山腰上出现一只红蚂蚁独行侠，显而易见，它斗志昂扬，要么是刚刚置一个对手于死地，要么就是刚刚投入战斗。大约是后者，因为它的四肢健全完好。它的母亲命令它要么手持盾牌胜利归来，要么躺在盾牌上被抬回来。它冲了过来，与对手拉开约半英寸的距离，等时机一到，就向黑武士扑了上去，一下咬住对方的右前腿，完全不顾对手会在自己身上哪个部位反咬一口。所以，此时是三只蚂蚁黏在一起生死搏命，好像产生出一种新的迷人的黏合剂似的，让所有的锁链和水泥都自愧不如。这时，我如果看到他们各自的军乐队，在突起的木片上演奏国歌来助阵，鼓舞那些奄奄一息的斗士，我也不会感到惊奇。甚至我自己都已经血脉偾张，把它们视为人类了。你越想就越觉得它们和人类没有什么不同。

The Battle of the Red and the Black Ants

By Henry David Thoreau

One day when I went out to my wood-pile, or rather my pile of stumps, I observed two large ants, the one red, the other much larger, nearly half an inch long, and black, fiercely contending with one another. Having once got hold they never let go, but struggled and wrestled and rolled on the chips incessantly. Looking further I was surprised to find that the chips were covered with such combatants, that it was not a "duellum" but a "bellum", a war between two races of ants, the red always pitted against the black, and frequently two red ones to one black. The legions of these Myrmidons covered all the hills and vales in my woodyard, and the ground was already strewn with the dead and dying, both red and black. It was the only battle which I have ever witnessed, the only battlefield I ever trod while the battle was raging; internecine war; the red republicans on the one hand and the black imperialists on the other hand. On every side they were engaged in deadly combat, yet without any noise that I could hear, and human soldiers never fought so resolutely.

    I watched a couple that were fast locked in each other's embraces in a little sunny valley amid the chips; now at noonday prepared to fight till the sun went down, or life went out. The smaller red champion had fastened himself like a vise on his adversary's front, and through all the tumblings on that field never for an instant ceased to gnaw at one of his feelers near the root, having already caused the other to go by the board; while the stronger black one dashed him from side to side, and, as I saw on looking nearer, had already divested him of several of his members. They fought with more pertinacity than bulldogs. Neither manifested the least disposition to retreat. It was evident that their battle-cry was "Conquer or die".

    In the meanwhile there came along a single red ant on the hillside of this valley, evidently full of excitement, who either had dispatched his foe, or had not yet taken part in the battle; probably the latter, for he had lost none of his limbs; whose mother had charged him to return with his shield or upon it. He drew near with rapid pace till he stood on his guard within half an inch of the combatants; then, watching his opportunity, he sprang upon the black warrior, and commenced his operations near the root of his right foreleg, leaving the foe to select among his own members; and so there were three united for life, as if a new kind of attraction had been invented which put all other locks and cements to shame.

I should not have wondered by this time to find that they had their respective musical bands stationed on some eminent chip, and playing their national airs the while, to excite the show and cheer the dying combatants. I was myself excited somewhat even as if they had been men. The more you think of it, the less the difference.

夏　夜

[美国] 安布罗斯·比尔斯

亨利·阿姆斯特朗已经下葬，这个事实不能证明他已经死了：他总是很难被说服。他的确已经下葬，他的所有感觉都迫使他承认。他的姿势——仰面朝天地躺着，双手交叉放在肚子上，手被什么东西绑着，不过，他不费吹灰之力就能改变局面——可是，他全身被束缚，现在是漆黑的夜晚，周围是深深的寂静，形成一个无法改变的证据体系，于是，他只好被迫接受了。

可是，死——不，他并没有死，他只是病得很严重，病入膏肓。他与其他病人一样冷漠，并没有太在意自己遭遇的不寻常的厄运。他不是哲学家——目前只是一个其貌不扬、稀松平常的人，天生具有病态的冷漠，那患得患失的器官已经迟钝。因此，他对眼前的未来没有特别的担心，他睡着了，亨利·阿姆斯特朗的一切都很平静。

但是他的头顶正在发生着一些什么。那是一个漆黑的夏夜，微弱的闪电时不时地闪亮，悄悄地点燃了西方的一朵低低的云，预示着一场暴风雨就要到来了。这些短促的、断断续续的灯光清晰而恐怖，照亮了墓地的纪念碑和墓碑，似乎还让它们翩翩起舞起来。在那个夜晚，在墓地里不可能有任何可靠的证人四处游荡，所以在那里挖掘亨利·阿姆斯特朗坟墓的三个人有理由感到十分安全。

掘坟人中的两个人是几英里以外的一所医学院的年轻学生；另外一个人叫杰斯，是一个体形彪悍的黑人。多年来，杰斯一直都受雇处理所有的墓地杂务，所以他最喜欢开的玩笑就是，他认识"这个地方的每一个人"。从他现在正在干的勾当的性质就可以推断出，这个地方的亡者不会像登记簿上记录的那么多。

墙外，在公用道路旁最远处的一块空地上，有一架小型马车在等候着……

挖掘工作并不困难：几个小时前被松散填满泥土的坟墓几乎没有阻力，很快就被铲掉了。把棺材从棺材架里拿出来没那么容易，但还是取出来了，因为是杰斯的杰作，他小心翼翼地拧开盖子，把它放在一边，露出身穿黑裤子和白衬衫的尸体。就在这时，空气突然燃烧起来，一声霹雳震撼了震惊的世界，亨利·阿姆斯特朗平静地坐了起来。这些人含混不清地一阵乱叫，惊恐地四散奔逃，因为世上没有任何东西能说服那两个人回来。但是杰斯却是另一个品种。

在天色泛白的时候，这两个学生在医学院相遇，惴惴不安的心情投射到了他们苍白憔悴的脸上，而刚刚的骇人经历使他们惊魂未定。

"你看见了吗？"一个人喊道。

"天哪！看见了——我们该怎么办？"

他们绕到大楼后面，看见一匹马拉着一辆轻型货车，拴在解剖室门口的门柱上。他们机械地走进房间，只见阴影里的长凳上坐着黑人杰斯。他站起身来，咧嘴笑着，眼睛和牙齿都在笑。"我在等着我的工钱。"他说。

亨利·阿姆斯特朗的尸体赤裸裸地躺在一张长桌上，头部明显被铁锹击打过，现在还沾满了血和泥土。

One Summer Night

By Ambrose Bierce

The fact that Henry Armstrong was buried did not seem to him to prove that he was dead: he had always been a hard man to convince. That he really was buried, the testimony of his senses compelled him to admit. His posture—flat upon his back, with his hands crossed upon his stomach and tied with something that he easily broke without profitably altering the situation—the strict confinement of his entire person, the black darkness and profound silence, made a body of evidence impossible to controvert and he accepted it without cavil.

But dead—no; he was only very, very ill. He had, withal, the invalid's apathy and did not greatly concern himself about the uncommon fate that had been allotted to him. No philosopher was he—just a plain, commonplace person gifted, for the time being, with a pathological indifference: the organ that he feared consequences with was torpid. So, with no particular apprehension for his immediate future, he fell asleep and all was peace with

Henry Armstrong.

But something was going on overhead. It was a dark summer night, shot through with infrequent shimmers of lightning silently firing a cloud lying low in the west and portending a storm. These brief, stammering illuminations brought out with ghastly distinctness the monuments and headstones of the cemetery and seemed to set them dancing. It was not a night in which any credible witness was likely to be straying about a cemetery, so the three men who were there, digging into the grave of Henry Armstrong, felt reasonably secure.

Two of them were young students from a medical college a few miles away; the third was a gigantic negro known as Jess. For many years Jess had been employed about the cemetery as a man-of-all-work and it was his favourite pleasantry that he knew "every soul in the place". From the nature of what he was now doing it was inferable that the place was not so populous as its register may have shown it to be.

Outside the wall, at the part of the grounds farthest from the public road, were a horse and a light wagon, waiting...

The work of excavation was not difficult: the earth with which the grave had been loosely filled a few hours before offered little resistance and was soon thrown out. Removal of the casket from its box was less easy, but it was taken out, for it was a perquisite of Jess, who carefully unscrewed the cover and laid it aside, exposing the body in black trousers and white shirt. At that instant the air sprang to flame, a cracking shock of thunder shook the stunned world and Henry Armstrong tranquilly sat up. With inarticulate cries the men fled in terror, each in a different direction. For nothing on earth could two of them have been persuaded to return. But Jess was of another breed.

In the grey of the morning the two students, pallid and haggard from anxiety and with the terror of their adventure still beating tumultuously in their blood, met at the medical college.

"You saw it?" cried one.

"God! yes—what are we to do?"

They went around to the rear of the building, where they saw a horse, attached to a light wagon, hitched to a gatepost near the door of the dissecting-room. Mechanically they entered the room. On a bench in the obscurity sat the negro Jess. He rose, grinning, all eyes and teeth. "I'm waiting for my pay." he said.

Stretched naked on a long table lay the body of Henry Armstrong, the head defiled with blood and clay from a blow with a spade.

骆驼为什么有驼峰

开辟鸿蒙之时,世界如此之新。动物们刚刚开始为人类干活的时候,有这么一只骆驼,因为不想干活,所以住在一个怒吼的沙漠的中部。此外,他本身就是个蠢货。他吃草棍、荆棘、柽柳、马利筋和刺草,成了最悠闲的动物,每当有人跟他说话,他只回答一声"哼!"就这么一声"哼!",就再没话了。

不久,一个周一的早晨,就有一匹马身背马鞍、嘴戴马嚼子来到骆驼面前,说道:"骆驼啊骆驼,出来像我们马一样小跑吧。"

"哼!"骆驼回答。于是马走了,把事情经过告诉了人。

不久,一条狗嘴里叼了根棍子来到骆驼面前,说道:"骆驼啊骆驼,像我们狗一样取东西送东西吧。"

"哼!"骆驼回答。于是狗走了,把事情经过告诉了人。

不久,公牛脖子上戴着轭来到骆驼面前,说道:"骆驼啊骆驼,像我们公牛一样犁地吧。"

"哼!"骆驼回答。于是公牛走了,把事情经过告诉了人。

这天晚上,人把马、狗和公牛召集到一起,说:"你们啊你们,我为你们感到万分难过(这个世界是如此之新什么的),可是那个沙漠里只会哼哼的东西不肯干活,否则他现在应该在这里。因此,我决定不去理他,你们必须加倍干活来弥补。"

听了这话,三个动物都义愤填膺起来(这个世界是如此之新什么的),在沙漠边缘进行了一场口水战,召开了一次南非土人会议、村务委员会、议事会。骆驼嚼着牛奶草,非常悠闲地走到他们面前,对他们嗤之以鼻,然后,他"哼"了一声就又扬长而去了。

不久,神怪在一阵尘土中翻滚而来,控制了整个沙漠地区(神怪总是这样出行的,因为这是他们的魔法),他停了下来,跟这三个动物进行了一场口水战,召开了一次议事会。

"统治整个沙漠的神怪,"马问道,"这个世界是如此之新什么的,不干活对吗?"

"当然不对。"神怪回答。

"那好,"马接着说,"在你怒吼的沙漠(他本身就是个蠢货)中部就有这么个东西,长脖子长腿的,从周一早晨一直到现在,一丁点儿活也没干,他不肯小跑。"

"哟!"神怪说着,吹了声口哨。"那是我的骆驼,看在阿拉伯全部黄金的面子上!他什么意见?"

"他说'哼!'"狗答道。"他不肯取东西运东西。"

"他还说什么了?"

"只是'哼'了一声,他不肯犁地。"公牛答道。

"很好,"神怪说,"你们稍等,我要对他说哼。"

神怪穿上了他的尘土披风,穿过沙漠向一个方向奔去,发现骆驼非常悠闲看着自己在池塘里的倒影。

"我身材修长、容光焕发的朋友。"神怪说。"这世界是如此之新什么的,我怎么听说你根本不干活呢?"

"哼!"骆驼说。

神怪坐了下来,手托着下巴,心中开始谋划一个伟大的魔法,而骆驼还是自顾自地看着自己在池塘里的倒影。

"由于你'太悠闲'了,从周一早晨开始,你给那三个动物增加了额外的活儿。"神怪嘴里说着,手托着下巴,心里继续谋划魔法。

"哼!"骆驼说。

"我要是你的话,就不会再哼哼。"神怪说。"你可能是以前哼哼得太多了。活跃分子,我要你干活。"

骆驼又"哼"了一声,可是他话音未落,就看见自己引以为豪的背在肿胀,肿胀成了一个懒散的大驼峰。

"你看见了吗?"神怪问。"由于你不干活,所以才惹得驼峰上身。今天是周四,而你从周一早晨,也就是开始干活的时间起,就没有干过活。现在你要去干活了。"

"我背上背个驼峰怎么干活?"

"驼峰是一份保证,"神怪说,"就因为你前三天没干活。驼峰保证你现在开始干三天的活儿,不吃东西,因为你可以靠驼峰活下去。你可别说我没帮你。现在走出沙漠,加入那三个动物的行列,规规矩矩的。自己哼给自己听吧!"

骆驼对自己哼着,哼哼唧唧地走远了,去加入那三个动物的行列了。也就是从那天开始,骆驼就一直长着驼峰(我们现在称之为"驼峰",是为了不伤他的感情)。可是,他根本就不可能把开辟鸿蒙时错过的那三天补回来,永远也学不会懂规矩。

骆驼的驼峰是丑陋的,你在动物园就可以看得清楚明白。我们身上的驼峰更丑陋,不论孩子还是大人,因为干活少,没有干足够的活,我们身上也会长驼峰——喜怒无常的驼峰——黑蓝相间的驼峰!我们头发脏乱,嘴里骂骂咧咧地从床上跳下来。

我们浑身颤抖,怒气冲冲地咕哝着,我们对着浴缸、靴子和玩具咆哮着。当我们身上长了驼峰——喜怒无常的驼峰——驼峰是黑蓝相间的,我们应该是有一个角落的(我知道你有)!治疗这种病的方法就是不能坐以待毙,或者愁眉不展地在壁炉旁捧着一本书。而是要拿起一把大锄头和大铁锹,挖到身体微微发汗。这样你就会发现太阳和风,还有花园里的神怪。去除了身体上的驼峰——可怕的驼峰,黑蓝相间的驼峰!我和你都会明白:如果我们干的活儿不够多,我们就会长驼峰——喜怒无常的驼峰,大人小孩都一样!

How the Camel Got His Hump

In the beginning of years, when the world was so new and all, and the Animals were just beginning to work for Man, there was a Camel, and he lived in the middle of a Howling Desert because he did not want to work; and besides, he was a Howler himself. So he ate sticks and thorns and tamarisks and milkweed and prickles, most excruciating idle; and when anybody spoke to him he said "Humph!" Just "Humph!" and no more.

Presently the Horse came to him on Monday morning, with a saddle on his back and a bit in his mouth, and said, "Camel, O Camel, come out and trot like the rest of us."

"Humph!" Said the Camel; and the Horse went away and told the Man.

Presently the Dog came to him, with a stick in his mouth, and said, "Camel, O Camel, come and fetch and carry like the rest of us."

"Humph!" Said the Camel; and the Dog went away and told the Man.

Presently the Ox came to him, with the yoke on his neck and

said, "Camel, O Camel, come and plough like the rest of us."

"Humph!" Said the Camel; and the Ox went away and told the Man.

At the end of the day the Man called the Horse and the Dog and the Ox together, and said, "Three, O Three, I'm very sorry for you (with the world so new-and-all); but that Humph-thing in the Desert can't work, or he would have been here by now, so I am going to leave him alone, and you must work double-time to make up for it."

That made the Three very angry (with the world so new-and-all), and they held a palaver, and an indaba, and a panchayat, and a pow-wow on the edge of the Desert; and the Camel came chewing on milkweed most excruciating idle, and laughed at them. Then he said "Humph!" and went away again.

Presently there came along the Djinn in charge of All Deserts, rolling in a cloud of dust (Djinns always travel that way because it is Magic), and he stopped to palaver and pow-wow with the Three.

"Djinn of All Deserts," said the Horse, "is it right for anyone to be idle, with the world so new-and-all?"

"Certainly not," said the Djinn.

"Well," said the Horse, "there's a thing in the middle of your Howling Desert (and he's a Howler himself) with a long neck and long legs, and he hasn't done a stroke of work since Monday morning. He won't trot."

"Whew!" said the Djinn, whistling, "that's my Camel, for all the gold in Arabia! What does he say about it?"

"He says 'Humph!'" said the Dog, "and he won't fetch and carry."

"Does he say anything else?"

"Only 'Humph!' And he won't plough." said the Ox.

"Very good." Said the Djinn. "I'll humph him if you will kindly wait a minute."

The Djinn rolled himself up in his dust-cloak, and took a bearing across the desert, and found the Camel most excruciatingly idle, looking at his own reflection in a pool of water.

"My long and bubbling friend," said the Djinn, "what's this I hear of your doing no work, with the world so new-and-all?"

"Humph!" Said the Camel.

The Djinn sat down, with his chin in his hand, and began to think a Great Magic, while the Camel looked at his own reflection in the pool of water.

"You've given the Three extra work ever since Monday morning, all on account of your 'excruciatingly idleness'," said the Djinn, and he went on thinking Magics, with his chin in his hand.

"Humph!" Said the Camel.

"I shouldn't say that again if I were you," said the Djinn, "you might say it once too often. Bubbles, I want you to work."

And the Camel said "Humph!" again, but no sooner had he said it than he saw his back, that he was so proud of, puffing up and puffing up into a great big lolloping humph.

"Do you see that?" said the Djinn. "That's your very own humph that you've brought upon your very own self by not working. Today is Thursday, and you've done no work since Monday, when the work began. Now you are going to work."

"How can I," said the Camel, "with this humph on my back?"

"That's made a-purpose," said the Djinn, "all because you missed those three days. You will be able to work now for three days without eating, because you can live on your humph, and don't you ever say I never did anything for you. Come out of the Desert and go to the Three, and behave. Humph yourself!"

And the Camel humphed himself, humph and all, and went away to join the three. And from that day to this the Camel always wears a humph (we call it "hump" now, not to hurt his feelings); but he has never yet caught up with the three days that he missed at the beginning of the world, and he has never yet learned how to behave.

The Camel's hump is an ugly lump, which well you may see at the Zoo; But uglier yet is the hump we get, From having too little to do. Kiddies and grown-ups, too. If we haven't enough to do, we get the hump—Cameelious hump—The hump that is black and blue! We climb out of bed with a frouzy head and a snarly-yarly voice.

  We shiver and scowl and we grunt and we growl, at our bath and our boots and our toys; And there ought to be a corner for me, (and I know there is one for you) When we get the hump — Cameelious hump—The hump that is black and blue! The cure for this ill is not to sit still, Or frowst with a book by the fire; But to take a large hoe and a shovel also, and dig till you gently perspire; And then you will find that the sun and the wind. And the Djinn of the Garden, too, have lifted the hump—the horrible hump. The hump that is black and blue! I get it as well as you—if I haven't enough to do—we all get hump—cameelious hump—kiddies and grown-ups, too!

房子上的藤蔓

[美国] 安布罗斯·比尔斯

在距离密苏里州的诺顿小镇大约三英里,通往梅斯维尔的路上,矗立着一座旧房子,最后被一个名叫哈丁的家族占用。自1886年以来,就没有人在里面住了,也没有人愿意再住在里面。随着时间的推移,以及居住在附近的人的冷待,它渐渐变成一个风景如画的废墟。一个不了解其历史的观察者很难把它归入"鬼屋"的范畴,但在该地区,这就是它的恶名。它的窗户没有玻璃,门廊也没有门;瓦屋顶有很宽的裂缝,由于没有刷过油漆,挡风板是暗灰色的。但是这些超自然的永恒迹象部分被隐藏起来,一根叶子茂密的大藤蔓覆盖了整幢房子,从而柔和了许多。这种藤——一种植物学家从未命名过的物种——是这个房子的故事中的重要组成部分。

哈丁一家包括罗伯特·哈丁、他的妻子马蒂尔达、她的妹妹茱莉亚·温特小姐和两个年幼的孩子。罗伯特·哈丁是一个沉默寡言、举止冷漠的人,他在附近与邻里没有交过朋友,而且显然不想交朋友。他大约四十岁,节俭勤劳,靠小农场为生,现在这个小农场已经长满了灌木和荆棘。他们的邻居们很忌讳他和他的小姨子的话题,他们似乎认为他们在一起的次数太多了——不完全是他们的错,因为在这些时候,他们显然是迎合闲言碎语的。密苏里州农村的道德准则是很严苛的。哈丁太太是一个温文尔雅、目光忧郁的女人,没有左脚。

1884年的某个时候,人们知道她去爱荷华州看望母亲。这就是人们询问时她丈夫的回答,而他说话的方式也不鼓励进一步提问。她再也没有回来过,两年后,没有卖掉他的农场或任何属于他的东西,没有指定一个代理人来照顾他的利益,也没有搬走他的家庭用品,哈丁和家人一起离开了这个国家。没人知道他去了哪里,当时也没人在意。很自然,这个地方的一切能搬走的东西很快都消失了,这座荒废的房子也因此成了"闹鬼"的地方。

大约四五年后的一个夏天的傍晚,诺顿·J.格鲁伯牧师和一位名叫凯悦的梅斯维尔律师骑马在哈丁家门前会面,他们有事情要讨论。他们把马拴好,然后进了哈丁家里,坐在门廊上说话。一说到这个地方阴沉的名声,他们还幽默了几句,说完就忘了。他们谈论他们的生意,一直谈到天快黑了。夜晚闷热难耐,空气污浊。

不久,两个人都惊奇地从座位上起身:一根长藤蔓覆盖着房子前面的一半,树枝从他们上面门廊的边缘垂了下来,明显地可以听见,也可以看见它们在颤抖,每根枝干和每片叶子都剧烈地摇晃着。

"我们要遭遇暴风雨了。"凯悦大声喊道。

格鲁伯什么也没说,只是默默地把另一个人的注意力引向了附近树木的枝叶,那里的枝叶一动不动,就连那几根枝条在晴空映衬下的纤细的枝头也一动不动。他们急忙走下台阶,来到原来的草坪上,仰起头望着那根葡萄藤,现在可以看见它的整个长度。它在继续剧烈地骚动着,但他们看不出任何令人不安的原因。

"我们走吧。"牧师说道。

他们离开了。他们忘记了自己一直在往相反的方向走,就一起骑马走了。他们去了诺顿,在那里他们把自己的奇怪经历告诉了几个为人谨慎的朋友。第二天晚上,大约在同一个时间,在另外两个名字不详的人的陪同下,他们又来到了哈丁家的门廊上,结果神秘的现象又一次出现了:经过最近距离的观察,发现藤蔓从树根到树梢都在剧烈地颤抖着,他们合力抱住树干,也没能让它静止下来。经过一个小时的观察,他们撤退了,据说至少比他们来的时候明白。

没过多久,整个邻里地区的好奇心就被这些奇特的事实唤起来了。白天和晚上,成群结队的人聚集在哈丁家"寻找线索"。似乎没有人找到,但目击者提到的证据是如此可信,没有人怀疑他们所证明的"显灵"的真实性。

有一天,有人提议,这提议要么是一个巧妙的灵感,要么就是一个有害的计划——似乎没人知道这个建议是从谁那里来的——去挖葡萄藤。经过一番激烈的辩论,这项工作终于完成了。除了树根什么也没有发现,但没有什么比这更奇怪的了!

这树干在地面上直径几英寸,在距离树干五到六英尺的地方,只有一个根向下笔直地延伸,扎进松散的土壤,然后分成根、纤维和细纤维,最奇怪的是都交织在一起。把它们小心翼翼地从土壤中解放出来时,显露出一种奇特的形态。在它们的分支的作用下,形成了一个紧凑的网络,在大小和形状上与人类的形象惊人地相似。头、躯干和四肢应有尽有,甚至手指和脚趾都有清楚的定义。许多人声称在代表头部的球状物质中的纤维的分布和排列中看到了一张怪诞的脸。这个人体形状是横着的,较小的根已经开始在胸部结合。

就与人类形态相似这一点而论,这一形象是不完美的。在距离其中一个膝盖大约十英寸的地方,形成腿的纤毛在生长过程中突然向后和向内翻了一倍。这个人没有左脚。

只有一个推论——一个显而易见的推论。但人们在随之而来的兴奋情绪里，就像没有能力的辅导员一样，提出了大量行动方案。这件事已由郡治安官解决，作为被遗弃遗产的合法保管人，县治安官下令更换树根，把挖出的泥土填回原处。

后来的调查只揭示了一个相关和重要的事实：哈丁夫人从未拜访过爱荷华州的亲戚，他们也不知道她有这么做的理由。

关于罗伯特·哈丁和他家里的其他人，全都一无所知。这所房子保留着它的恶名，但是重新种植的藤蔓有条不紊、举止得体，就像一个神经紧张的人可能希望在一个愉快的夜晚坐在藤蔓下面似的，当蝈蝈摆脱了它们远古的启示，远处的北美夜鹰表达了它应该做些什么的想法。

A Vine on a House

By Ambrose Bierce

About three miles from the little town of Norton in Missouri, on the road leading to Maysville, stands an old house that was last occupied by a family named Harding. Since 1886 no one has lived in it, nor is anyone likely to live in it again. Time and the disfavor of persons dwelling thereabout are converting it into a rather picturesque ruin. An observer unacquainted with its history would hardly put it into the category of "haunted houses", yet in all the region round such is its evil reputation. Its windows are without glass, its doorways without doors; there are wide breaches in the shingle roof, and for lack of paint the weatherboarding is a dun gray. But these unfailing signs of the supernatural are partly concealed and greatly softened by the abundant foliage of a large vine overrunning the entire structure. This vine—of a species which no botanist has ever been able to name—has an important part in the story of the house.

The Harding family consisted of Robert Harding, his wife

Matilda, Miss Julia Went, who was her sister, and two young children. Robert Harding was a silent, cold-mannered man who made no friends in the neighborhood and apparently cared to make none. He was about forty years old, frugal and industrious, and made a living from the little farm which is now overgrown with brush and brambles. He and his sister-in-law were rather tabooed by their neighbors, who seemed to think that they were seen too frequently together—not entirely their fault, for at these times they evidently did not challenge observation. The moral code of rural Missouri is stern and exacting. Mrs. Harding was a gentle, sad-eyed woman, lacking a left foot.

At some time in 1884 it became known that she had gone to visit her mother in Iowa. That was what her husband said in reply to inquiries, and his manner of saying it did not encourage further questioning. She never came back, and two years later, without selling his farm or anything that was his, or appointing an agent to look after his interests, or removing his household goods, Harding, with the rest of the family, left the country. Nobody knew whither he went; nobody at that time cared. Naturally, whatever was movable about the place soon disappeared and the deserted house became "haunted" in the manner of its kind.

One summer evening, four or five years later, the Rev. J. Gruber, of Norton, and a Maysville attorney named Hyatt met on horseback in front of the Harding place. Having business matters to discuss, they hitched their animals and going to the house sat on the porch to talk. Some humorous reference to the somber reputation of the place was made and forgotten as soon as uttered, and they talked of their business affairs until it grew almost dark. The evening was oppressively warm, the air stagnant.

Presently both men started from their seats in surprise: a long vine that covered half the front of the house and dangled its branches from the edge of the porch above them was visibly and audibly agitated, shaking violently in every stem and leaf.

"We shall have a storm." Hyatt exclaimed.

Gruber said nothing, but silently directed the other's attention to the foliage of adjacent trees, which showed no movement, even the delicate tips of the boughs silhouetted against the clear sky were motionless. They hastily passed down the steps to what had been a lawn and looked upward at the vine, whose entire length was now visible. It continued in violent agitation, yet they could discern no disturbing cause.

"Let us leave." said the minister.

And leave they did. Forgetting that they had been traveling in opposite directions, they rode away together. They went to Norton, where they related their strange experience to several discreet friends. The next evening, at about the same hour, accompanied by two others whose names are not recalled, they were again on the porch of the Harding house, and again the mysterious phenomenon occurred: the vine was violently agitated while under the closest scrutiny from root to tip, nor did their combined strength applied to the trunk serve to still it. After an hour's observation they retreated, no less wise, it is thought, than when they had come.

No great time was required for these singular facts to rouse the curiosity of the entire neighborhood. By day and by night crowds of persons assembled at the Harding house "seeking a sign". It does not appear that any found it, yet so credible were the witnesses mentioned that none doubted the reality of the "manifestations" to which they testified.

By either a happy inspiration or some destructive design, it was one day proposed—nobody appeared to know from whom the suggestion came—to dig up the vine, and after a good deal of debate this was done. Nothing was found but the root, yet nothing could have been more strange!

For five or six feet from the trunk, which had at the surface of the ground a diameter of several inches, it ran downward, single and straight, into a loose, friable earth; then it divided and subdivided into rootlets, fibers and filaments, most curiously interwoven. When carefully freed from soil they showed a singular formation. In their ramifications and doublings back upon themselves they made a compact network, having in size and shape an amazing resemblance to the human figure. Head, trunk and limbs were there; even the fingers and toes were distinctly defined;

and many professed to see in the distribution and arrangement of the fibers in the globular mass representing the head a grotesque suggestion of a face. The figure was horizontal, the smaller roots had begun to unite at the breast.

In point of resemblance to the human form this image was imperfect. At about ten inches from one of the knees, the cilia forming that leg had abruptly doubled backward and inward upon their course of growth. The figure lacked the left foot.

There was but one inference—the obvious one. But in the ensuing excitement as many courses of action were proposed as there were incapable counselors. The matter was settled by the sheriff of the county, who as the lawful custodian of the abandoned estate ordered the root replaced and the excavation filled with the earth that had been removed.

Later inquiry brought out only one fact of relevancy and significance: Mrs. Harding had never visited her relatives in Iowa, nor did they know that she was supposed to have done so.

Of Robert Harding and the rest of his family nothing is known. The house retains its evil reputation, but the replanted vine is as orderly and well-behaved a vegetable as a nervous person could wish to sit under of a pleasant night, when the katydids grate out their immemorial revelation and the distant whippoorwill signifies his notion of what ought to be done about it.

最好的朋友

[英国] 杰克·奥尔索普

家里没人,这一目了然:那些从信箱凸出来的报纸可以证明主人不在家。

"快点儿!我们闯进去!"

"我认为我们不应该这么做。这和偷苹果可是两码事。"

"你害怕了?胆小鬼!"

"谁是胆小鬼?我证明给你看。"

迪吉比金杰高,所以他能伸手打开窗户。男孩们爬了进去,东张西望。然后他们听到了一辆车停在屋外的刺耳刹车声。他们尽可能快地跑。金杰跑了,但迪吉被绊倒了。警察抓住迪吉的衣领,把他带到警察局。警察问了他好几个小时,他们想知道另外一个男孩的名字,但迪吉没有告诉他们。

与此同时,金杰坐在家里,心惊胆战,他随时都可能听到警察在敲他的门。但是他不必担心。他的朋友迪吉什么也没说。迪吉被判入狱约一年。当他出来的时候,他知道他的父母并不需要他,所以他决定去看他的老朋友金杰。金杰没有去监狱看望他。也许他的父母曾告诉过他不许去。

迪吉没有认出开门的那个女人。

"哦,他们已经不住在这里了。我想他们搬到了伯明翰,但我不是很确定。抱歉。"

站台上人山人海,此时是交通高峰期,一群商务人士,有男有女,正在等火车把他们送回他们在郊区舒适的家。在等候的乘客中有一个高个子男人,身穿一件昂贵的大衣。他的脸胖胖的,看上去生活得很好,只吃最好的食物。他站在一张写着"当心扒手"的警示牌下。一个体型瘦长的红发男人迅速穿过人群。他朝那个脑满肠肥的高个子男人走去,撞了他一下,然后迅速地溜走了。不幸的是,一位铁路警察却把这一切尽收眼底。他抓住了那个瘦长男人的衣领,把他拖回那个高个子男人站着的地方。

"对不起,先生,"警察说,"请您检查一下您的口袋好吗?"

"天哪!我的钱包!我的钱包不见了。"

警察抓住那个瘦长男人的衣领把他拉了上来。"快点儿,拿出来吧!"

扒手把钱包拿出来交给了警察。

"这是你的钱包吗?"

"对,是我的!看。那是我名字的缩写。"

他低头看看那个小偷,眼里充满了厌恶。就在那一刻,尽管迪吉已经二十五年没有见过他了,但他认出了他的童年朋友,金杰,就是以前和他一起闯进过一幢房子的那个人,当时警察来了,然后……

金杰的眼睛一直盯着地面,他没有兴趣盯着那个他刚想偷窃的人的脸看。

"先生,您想控告这个人吗?"警察问。一阵沉默。

"当然,警官。"迪吉说。"我们必须给这些小偷一个教训。"

扒手耸了耸肩。他甚至不恨那个商人。当警察把他带走时，他对自己说世界就是这样。

此时，迪吉，那位成功的商人，上了火车，他对自己身为一个好公民履行的职责感到心满意足。

Best Friends

By Jake Allsop

Clearly there was nobody at home: those newspapers sticking out of the letterbox are a sure sign that the owners are away.

"Come on! Let's break in!"

"I don't think we should. It's not like stealing apples."

"Are you afraid? Chicken!"

"Who's chicken? I'll show you."

Being taller than Ginger, Deggy was able to reach up and open the window. The boys climbed in and looked around. Then they heard the screech of breaks as a car pulled up outside the house. They ran as fast as they could. Ginger got away, but Deggy tripped and fell. The policeman grabbed Deggy by the collar and took him to the police station. They questioned him for hours and hours. They wanted to know the other boy's name, but he didn't tell them.

Meanwhile, Ginger sat at home, terrified. He expected at any moment to hear policemen knocking on his door. But he needn't have worried. His friend Deggy said nothing. He was sent to prison or a year. When he got out, he knew that his parents did not want him, so he decided to go and see his old friend, Ginger. Ginger had not visited him in prison. Perhaps his parents had told him not to.

Deggy did not recognize the woman who opened the door.

"Oh, they don't live here any more. I think they moved to Birmingham, but I am not sure. Sorry."

The platform was crowed. It was the rush hour, and a crowd of business men and women were waiting for the train to take them back to their comfortable homes in the suburbs. Among the waiting passengers was a tall man in an expensive overcoat. He had the fat face of a man who lives well and eats only the best food. He was standing under the notice that said "Beware of Pickpockets". A slim red-haired man was moving quickly through the crowd. He worked his way over to the tall well-fed man, bumped into him and then slipped away quickly. Unfortunately for him, a railway policeman had seen the whole thing. He grabbed the slim man by the collar, and dragged him to where the tall man was standing.

"Excuse me, sir," the policeman said, "but would you be good enough to check your pockets."

"Good heavens! My wallet! I can't find my wallet."

The policeman pulled the slim man up by his collar. "Come on, let's have it!"

The pickpocket took the wallet out and handed it over the

policeman.

"Is this your wallet, sir?"

"Yes, it is! Look. Those are my initials."

He looked down at the thief, his eyes filled with disgust. At that moment, despite the fact that he had not seen him in twenty-five year, he recognized his childhood friend, Ginger, the one he had been with when they had broken into a house and the police had come and…

Ginger kept his eyes fixed on the ground. He had no interest in staring into the face of the man he had just tried to rob.

"Do you want to press charges against this man, sir?" The policeman asked. There was a moment's silence.

"Of course, officer," Deggy said. "We must teach these thieves a lesson."

The pickpocket shrugged his shoulders. He didn't even hate the businessman. That's the way the world is, he thought to himself as the policeman took him away.

Meanwhile, Deggy, the successful businessman, had boarded his train, satisfied that he had done his duty as a good citizen.

石狮子

从前有两兄弟，他们的父亲过世了，他们跟母亲一起住在一个农场的大房子里。哥哥聪明、自私，弟弟却善良、温和。哥哥不喜欢弟弟，因为弟弟太老实，讨价还价时占不上便宜。于是，有一天，他对弟弟说："你必须离开这个家，我不能再养你了。"

就这样，弟弟整理了自己的全部行李，然后向母亲告别。母亲听了哥哥的所作所为后说："我要跟你走，离开这里，儿子，我不愿意跟你哥哥这样铁石心肠的人住在一起。"

第二天，母亲和弟弟就一起出了门。快到夜里的时候，他们来到一座小山的山脚下，来到一个小屋前。小屋门后有一把斧子，屋里什么都没有。他们凑合地做了顿晚饭，就在小屋里过了夜。

清晨，他们看到小屋旁有一座大森林，于是，儿子拿起斧头上山坡砍了好多木柴，背到山那边的小镇。他很快就把木柴卖掉了，开心地买回了食物和衣服，让母亲和自己舒服些。

"母亲，既然我挣的够我们俩生活，我们将来会幸福的。"他说。

有一天，在寻找细木的时候，弟弟走得比以前远。他爬上了陡峭的山坡，突然发现了一个石头刻的狮子。

"哦，"弟弟想着，"这一定是这座山的守护神。我明天早晨一定要给他进贡。"

那天夜里,他带了两根蜡烛,来到石狮子面前。他把两根蜡烛点着,在石狮子两边各放了一根,请求继续行好运。

就在他站在那里的时候,石狮子张开石头刻的嘴问道:"你在这里干什么?"

弟弟告诉石狮子,哥哥对自己是多么残忍,自己和母亲被迫离开家,现在住在山脚下的小屋里。石狮子听了这番讲述以后,说道:"你明天带一个木桶来,放到我嘴的下面,我会给你装满金子。"

第二天,弟弟带来了木桶。

"你要非常小心,桶快满的时候,告诉我。"石狮子说。"因为只要有一块金子掉到地上,你就会大祸临头。"

弟弟小心翼翼、不折不扣地按照石狮子的告诫去做,很快,他就提着满满一桶金子走在了回家的路上,见到了母亲。他们现在富了,所以买了一个美丽的农场,搬到那里去住。

铁石心肠的哥哥终于听说他们交了好运。母亲和弟弟走后,他就结了婚。所以他带着妻子来看弟弟。很快,他就听说了他们好运的来龙去脉,听说金子都是石狮子给他们的。

"我也要试一试。"他说。

他和妻子去了母亲和弟弟曾经住过的小屋,在那里过了一夜。

第二天早晨,他带着一个木桶出发,去拜访石狮子。他告诉石狮子此行的目的以后,石狮子说:"我会满足你的愿望,可是你一定要非常小心,桶快满的时候告诉我,因为哪怕有一小块金子掉到地上,你也肯定会大祸临头的。"

由于哥哥太贪心,所以他一直在摇木桶,让金子装得更实些。木桶快满的时候,他也没有像弟弟所做的那样,告诉石狮子,因为他想尽可能地多得。

突然，一块金子掉到了地上。

"哦，"石狮子喊道，"一块金子卡到了我的嗓子里，你伸手把它掏出来。这是最大的那块金子。"

贪心的哥哥立刻把手伸进了石狮子的嘴里，可是石狮子却一口咬住，合上了嘴巴！石狮子不肯放他走，哥哥就被困在那里，木桶里的金子也变成了土和石头。

夜晚来临，丈夫未归，妻子心急如焚，出去寻找。最后，她发现了被石狮子紧紧咬住的他，疲惫不堪、又冷又饿的他。

"唉！"她说。"我真希望我们没有出来搞什么金子。小屋里没有食物，我们会饿死的。"

石狮子听到了他们说的每一句话，看到他们倒霉，他很高兴，不禁哈哈大笑，嘲笑起他们来。他笑的时候张开了嘴，在他还没来得及再次闭嘴之前，贪心的哥哥迅速抽回了手。夫妻二人挣脱了石狮子，喜出望外地又去了弟弟家。弟弟为他们难过，给了他们足够的钱买了幢房子。

弟弟和母亲在美丽的家里过着无比幸福的生活，可是他们一直没有忘却这山坡上带给他们好运的石狮子。

The Stone Lion

Once there were two brothers who lived with their mother in a large house on a farm. Their father was dead. The older brother was clever and selfish, but the younger was kind and gentle. The older brother did not like the younger because he was so honest that he never could get the best of a bargain. One day he said to him: "You must go away. I cannot afford to support you any longer."

So the younger brother packed all his belongings, and went to bid his mother good-bye. When she heard what the older brother had done, she said, "I will go with you, my son. I will not live here any longer with so hard-hearted a man as your brother."

The next morning the mother and the younger brother started out together. Toward night when they reached the foot of the hill, they came to a hut with nothing in it except an ax which stood behind the door. But they managed to get their supper and stayed in the hut all night.

In the morning they saw that on the side of the hill near the hut was a great forest. The son took the ax, went up on the hillside and chopped enough wood for a load to carry to the town on the other side of the hill. He easily sold it, and with a happy heart brought back food and some clothing to make his mother and himself comfortable.

"Now, Mother," he said, "I can earn enough to keep us both, and we shall be happy here together."

One day, in search of timber, the boy went farther up the hill than he had ever gone before. As he climbed up the steep hillside, he suddenly came upon a lion carved from stone.

"Oh," thought the boy, "this must be the guardian spirit of the mountain. I will make him some offering tomorrow morning without fail."

That night he bought two candles and carried them to the lion. He lighted them, put one on each side of the lion, and asked that his own good fortune might continue.

As he stood there, suddenly, the lion opened his great stone mouth and said: "What are you doing here?"

The boy told him how cruel the elder brother had been; how the mother and himself had been obliged to leave home and live in a hut at the foot of the hill. When he had heard all of the story, the lion said: "If you will bring a bucket here tomorrow and put it under my mouth, I will fill it with gold for you."

The next day the boy brought the bucket.

"You must be very careful to tell me when it is nearly full," said the lion. "For if even one piece of gold should fall to the ground, great trouble would be in store for you."

The boy was very careful to do exactly as the lion told him, and soon he was on his way home to his mother with a bucketful of gold. They were so rich now that they bought a beautiful farm and went there to live.

At last the hard-hearted brother heard of their good fortune. He had married since his mother and brother had gone away, so he took his wife and went to pay a visit to his younger brother. It was not long before he had heard the whole story of their good fortune, and how the lion had given them all the gold.

"I will try that, too," he said.

He and his wife went to the same hut his brother had lived in, and there they passed the night.

The next morning he started out with a bucket to visit the stone lion. When he had told the lion his errand, the lion said, "I will grant your wish, but you must be very careful to tell me when the bucket is nearly full; for if even one little piece of gold touches the ground, great misery will surely fall upon you."

Now the elder brother was so greedy that he kept shaking the bucket to get the gold pieces closer together. And when the bucket was full he did not tell the lion, as the younger brother had done, for he wanted all he could possibly get.

Suddenly one of the gold pieces fell upon the ground.

"Oh," cried the lion, "a big piece of gold is stuck in my throat. Put your hand in and get it out. It is the largest piece of all."

The greedy man thrust his hand at once into the lion's mouth and the lion snapped his jaws together! And there the man stayed, for the lion would not let him go. And the gold in the bucket turned into earth and stones.

When night came and the husband did not return, the wife became anxious and went out to search for him. At last she found him with his arm held fast in the lion's mouth. He was tired and cold and hungry.

"Alas!" she said, "I wish we had not tried to get the gold. There is no food in the hut for us and we shall have to die."

The lion was listening to all that was said, and he was so pleased at their misfortune that he began to laugh at them, "Ha, ha, ha!" As he laughed, he opened his mouth and the greedy man quickly drew out his hand, before the lion had a chance to close his jaws again. They were glad enough to get away, and they went to their brother's house once more. The brother was sorry for them and gave them enough money to buy a home.

The younger brother and his mother lived very happily in their beautiful home, but they always remembered the Stone Lion on the hillside, who gave them their good fortune.

为什么海水是咸的

很久以前,在一个非常非常遥远的地方,住着兄弟俩。两兄弟一个腰缠万贯,一个一贫如洗。有钱的哥哥住在一个小岛上,是个盐商,卖了很多年的盐,赚了很多钱。他的弟弟穷到妻儿都是吃了上顿没下顿的地步。

他妻子说:"我们将来可怎么办呢?你是想要我们和孩子去死吗?一点儿吃的都没有了,你为什么就不能向你哥哥开口借点儿钱呢?"

"我哥哥爱财如命,我可以肯定他一分都不会借给我,他可能会给我一把盐,不过,我会去见他。"

他上了小船,向他哥哥住的小岛划去。

他发现他那有钱的哥哥在家数钱呢。

"什么情况啊?你怎么到这里来了?"

"求求你,哥哥,我家里没吃的了,求你从数的这些钱里拿出一块金子给我吧。"

"那可不行,那是我的钱。你太懒了,你为什么不出去工作呢?"

"我也试着找过工作,可没找着。现在我家里已经没有面包给孩子吃啦。"

"我不会给你钱的,可我会给你面包。我给你一条面包,你就走,不要再回来了,怎么样?"

"好的,把面包给我吧。"

有钱的哥哥丢给他一条面包,他走了。

在回家的路上,他碰到一位老人坐在路边。

"你手里拿的是什么?"老人问道。"是面包吗?我已经整整两天没吃东西了。"

"这是我准备给自己和孩子吃的,可我不愿意看到别人挨饿。来,我给你切一片。"

他切了一片面包递给老人。老人谢过他就吃开了。吃完以后,老人说道:"现在,让我来为你做点事,我要带你去兔子的家,他们住在地下。如果你把面包给他们看,他们就会想从你手里买下来,可是你不要让他们付你钱,你跟他们要放在门后的小磨。按照我说的去做,你就会富起来。等你回来以后,我会教你怎么使用小磨。"

老人把他领进了一座森林。他指给他看地下的一个洞穴。这个洞穴看起来像一个大兔子挖的。进洞以后,豁然开朗,可以看见一扇小石门。

"那就是兔子的家。进去,把门打开。我等你出来。"老人说道。

穷弟弟进洞,把门打开,走了进去。门里的光线很暗,一时间,他什么都看不见。接着,他看得更清楚了些,他看见了许多小兔子,他们向他围拢过来。

"那是什么?"其中一个小兔子问道。"是白面包吗?请把它送给我们,或者卖给我们。"

"我们会给你金银的。"另一个小兔子说。

"不,"穷人说,"我不要金也不要银。把架在门后的那盘旧磨给我,我就把面包给你们。"

起初,他们不愿意用磨交换面包,于是他转过身去。

但是一些小兔子开始哭泣："把旧磨给他，我们根本就用不着。只有好人才可以让它发挥作用。"

然后他们把小磨给了他。他把它夹在腋下，走出仙境。他发现老人在等他。

"就是这样。"老人说。"它应该这样用。只有好人才能用。除了你，谁用也不行。"

当穷人到家的时候已经很晚了。

"你跑到哪里去了？"他的妻子问道。"房子里没有火也没有食物。孩子们冷，哭着要吃东西。你拿的是什么？看起来像一盘旧磨。"

"这就是一盘磨。"他说。"现在看好了。说你想要什么，你就会拥有什么。"

他把磨放在桌子上，开始转动。从小磨里磨出来的是烤火用的劈柴、照明和烹饪用的油、衣服、玉米和许多其他的好东西。

"这是一盘神磨。"他的妻子说。"现在我们有钱了。"

"是的，可是不能让任何人知道。我们必须把它藏起来，只有在没有人看见的时候才能用。"

穷人很快就和他哥哥一样有钱了。他没有把所有的好东西留给自己的家人独享。他把很多东西给了穷朋友。

他哥哥听说以后，自言自语地说："我不知道为什么我的弟弟发财了。我必须找到他发财的原因。"

他花了很长一段时间试图找出原因，却没找到。有一天，他给了一个仆人一些钱，命令他晚上去暗中窥探他弟弟家。那天晚上，仆人透过窗户朝屋里看，看到全家人围着磨站着，磨在转。他回去汇报了他的所见所闻。

第二天，哥哥划着小船过了河。他对弟弟说："我知道你现在很有钱,我还知道原因,你有一个小神磨。把磨卖给我。你想要多少钱?"

"我不能卖。"穷人回答。"它永远不能离开我的手。老人说过:'如果你把它卖了,或者把它送给别人,必将大祸临头。'这是他的原话。"

然后有钱的哥哥划船离开了弟弟的家。但后来,一个漆黑的夜晚,他又潜了回来,蹑手蹑脚地走进兄弟的家,偷走了磨。他很快就把它带到了海上,他的小船在那里等着。然后向他的小岛驶去。

但是坏哥哥非常想让磨转起来。他等不及回到家。当他还在船上航行时,他试图使它发挥作用。

"盐。"他说。"盐是我卖的,盐是我想要的。"然后他开始转动小磨。

然后,盐粒从磨里磨了出来。他哈哈大笑,唱起歌来。大量的盐磨出来了,小船装满了。船的水位越来越低。他试图把一些盐扔进海里,但更多的盐磨出来了,很多。他笑不出来也唱不下去了。接着他开始害怕起来。

更多的盐从磨里磨了出来,很快船里就装满了盐。然后海水灌了进来,海水淹没了小船。小船开始下沉,带着小偷和神磨沉到了海底。

在海底,神磨还在不停地转动,磨出越来越多的盐。

(有些人说)这就是为什么海水是咸的的原因。

The Magic Mill

A long time ago, far, far away, there lived two brothers. One of them was quite rich, the other was very poor. The rich brother lived on a little island, he was a seller of salt. He had sold salt for many years and had got a great deal of money. The other brother was so poor that he had not got enough food for his wife and children.

His wife said, "What will happen to us? Do you want me and the children to die? There is nothing to eat. Why don't you go and ask your brother for some money."

"My brother loves his money very much. I'm sure that he will not give me any. Perhaps he will want to give me a handful of salt. But I will go and see him."

He got into his boat and sailed across to the island where his brother lived.

He found his rich brother at home, counting his money.

"What is the matter? Why have you come here?"

"Please, brother, I have no food in my house. Please give me one of those gold pieces you are counting."

"No. These are mine. You are very lazy. Why do you not go and work?"

"I have tried to find some work, but I cannot. Now there is no bread in my house for my children."

"I will not give you any money, but I'll give you some bread. If I give you a loaf of bread, will you go away and not come back?"

"Yes. Please give me the bread."

The rich man threw a loaf of bread to him, and he went away.

While he was on his way to his house, he came to an old man sitting by the side of the road.

"What is that you are carrying?" said the old man. "Is it bread? I have not had anything to eat for two days."

"The bread is for my children and I. But I don't want to see others having no food to eat. Come on, I will cut you a piece of it for you."

He cut a piece of the loaf and gave it to the old man, who thanked him and began to eat. When he had finished, the old man said, "Now I will do something for you. I will show you the home of the fairies who live underground. If you show them the bread, they will want to buy it from you. But do not let them give you any money. Ask them for the little mill that stands behind their door. Do as I say, and you will become rich. When you come back, I will show you how to use it."

The old man then led him into a wood. He pointed to a hole in the ground. It looked like the hole made by a big rabbit. Inside, the hole grew bigger and a little stone door could be seen.

"That is the fairies' home. Get in and open the door. I will wait until you come out." said the old man.

The poor man got into the hole, opened the door, and went in. It was dark inside the door: for some time he could see nothing. Then, when he could see more clearly, he saw many little fairies: they came and stood round him.

"What is that?" said one of them. "Is it white bread? Please give it to us, or sell it to us."

"We will give you gold and silver for it," said another.

"No," said the poor man. "I don't want gold or silver. Give me that old mill that stands behind the door, and I will give you the loaf of bread."

At first they did not want to give him the mill for the bread, so he turned away.

But some of the fairies began to cry, "Let him have the old mill. We never use it now. And only good people can make it work."

Then they gave him the mill. He put it under his arm and went out of fairy-land. He found the old man waiting for him.

"That is it," the old man said. "This is how to use it. Only good people can use it. You must never let any other person use it."

It was quite late when the poor man reached home.

"Where have you been?" Said his wife. "There is no fire and no food in the house. The children are cold and crying for food. What is that you are carrying. It looks like an old mill."

"It is a mill," he said. "Now watch. Say what you want, and you will have it."

He put the mill on the table and began to turn it. Out of the little mill came wood for the fire, oil for lighting and cooking, clothes, corn, and many other good things.

"It is a magic mill," said his wife. "Now we are rich."

"Yes, but no-one must know about it. We must hide it and use it only when no-one is watching."

The poor man soon became as rich as his brother. He did not keep all the good things for his own family. He gave many things to poor friends.

When his brother heard about this, he said to himself, "I do not know why my brother has become rich. I must find the reason for his riches."

For a long time he tried to find the reason, but he could not. But one day he gave a servant some money and ordered him to watch the house of his brother at night. That night, the servant looked through the window and saw the family standing round the mill, which was working. He went back and told what he had seen.

The next day the brother got in his boat and sailed across the water. He said to his brother, "I see that you are now quite rich, and I know the reason. You have a little magic mill. Sell it to me. How much money do you want for it?"

"I cannot sell it," said the poor man. "It must never leave my hands. The old man said, 'There will be great danger if you sell it or give it to any other person.' That is what he said."

Then the rich brother sailed away home. But later, one dark night, he came back, went very quietly into the house, and stole the mill. He quickly carried it to the sea, where his boat was waiting. Then he sailed away to his island.

But the bad brother wanted very much to make the mill work. He did not wait until he reached home. While he was sailing in the boat, he tried to make it work.

"Salt," he said. "Salt is what I sell, and salt is what I want." Then he began to turn the mill.

Then salt bean to come out of the mill. He laughed and began to sing. Masses of salt came out and began to fill the boat. The boat became low in the water. He tried to throw some of the salt into the sea. But more came in, masses of it. He stopped laughing and singing. Then he began to be afraid.

More salt came out of the mill, and soon the boat was full of it. Then water came in and filled the boat. The boat went down, down to the bottom of the sea, carrying with it the thief and the magic mill.

There, at the bottom of the sea, the mill is still turning, making more and more salt.

That is the reason (some people say) why the water of the sea is salty.

雪 人

在一个星期六的下午,大雪纷飞,一个小男孩和他爸爸清理暴风雪到来时落下的树叶和树枝。他们停下来稍事休息,静静地坐看纷纷飘落的雪花。

他们两个从头到脚都裹得严严实实的。妈妈坚持说:"如果你们感冒了,还得我来照顾。"于是他们乖乖地戴上了围巾和帽子,走出了家门。

"爸爸,我朋友告诉我每片雪花都是不一样的。"小男孩说。

爸爸回答说:"我认为你朋友说的是对的。"

一片寂静。

"我们是怎么知道的?"这个男孩问。

爸爸笑眯眯地转过头来看着他儿子说道:"我们就是知道。"

"可是,对我来说它们看起来都一样。"小男孩补充道。

这时,爸爸觉得有必要给儿子一个含义更为深远的答案,让他更为满意的答案,一个能够让他在多年以后依然能够想起此时此刻的答案。

"儿子,雪花跟人是一样的。上帝把我们创造成不同的人,我们每个人在某个特殊的方面都是独一无二的。我们怎么知道我们是独一无二的呢?我们就是知道。"爸爸意识到这根本不是一个好的答案。这个答案就落入了"因为我说是这样,所以就是这样"的套路,于是爸爸补充道:"我们现在就可以做个实验。"

小男孩站了起来,伸出一只手,然后观察落在手套上的雪花。小男孩说:"它们确实都不一样,像人似的。"然而他又生出了一个大问题,"他们在一起的时候很美丽,那么他们为什么不好好相处呢?"

爸爸问:"你是说雪花吗?"

"不是,我说的是人,爸爸。为什么人们不好好相处呢?如果人如你说的那样,像雪花一样独一无二又各有特色,那他们为什么不好好相处呢?"

哇,这真是一个好问题,一个配得到精彩答案的问题。

"我的意思是,当你看手套上的雪花时,它们是不一样的。但当你看院子里堆在一起的雪花时,它们却又是一样的。它们在一起的时候更美丽。"

爸爸坐在这里思考了一会儿,说道:"选择权。"

"选择权?"小男孩问。

"上帝给我们的一个最伟大的礼物就是'选择权',不同的我们却都有共同的选择权。我们可以选择做什么、穿什么、住哪里、如何对待别人。"

"这么说选择权是一个坏事了?"男孩问道。

"哦,不。当我们选择做错事情的时候,它才是一件坏事情。"

男孩问道:"那我们又怎么知道什么是对,什么是错呢?"

爸爸环顾四周,努力建立这一刻的基础。是的,很容易回到"我们就是这样"的套路中去。但是他现在的处境特别。他得到了一个为儿子的信念建立基础的机会。爸爸在心里寻找正确答案的时候,雪里的脚紧张地动来动去。

"我们就把这雪比作世界上的所有人。他们在一起时很美丽,他们得到了这个礼物,拥有选择权,他们意识到在一起工作时会做得很好,所以他们开始建造。"

爸爸俯下身来,把雪分成了两片。

"双方都知道他们是不同的。一方说,让我们一起努力,求同存异,做一些对世界有益的事情。而另一方也是这样说的,但在怎么做时意见不能达成一致,因此双方就成了对立的了。"

爸爸停了一会儿,然后看着儿子问:"你现在明白了吗?"

"明白了,我想是明白了。"儿子答道。

然后,爸爸没再说话,继续铲雪。他在一边堆了三个大雪球,在另一边堆了几个小雪球。

"哪边是对的?"他问儿子。

儿子看了看两边,想不出答案:"爸爸我不知道。"

然后爸爸把三个大雪球一个放到一个上面。

"原来是一个雪人呀!"儿子大声喊道。

"现在哪边做得对?"

"雪人这边。"儿子热情洋溢地回答道。

爸爸说:"对,所有的人应该团结一致,同时意识到彼此的特别之处,所以他们共同努力创造出人类。"

男孩接着站了起来,抱起一堆小雪球,开始一个一个地把它们扔向另外一个小雪堆。

"你在干什么?"爸爸问。

"这就是当人们不一起工作的时候所发生的事情,他们之间会发生一场战争。"儿子答道。

爸爸大吃一惊。他站起来，举起儿子，紧紧地抱着他。他在儿子耳边轻声说道："我向上帝祈祷，你会学会与别人一起工作和生活。"

　　儿子舒舒服服地依偎在爸爸的怀里，爸爸的双臂保护着他。儿子看着爸爸说："我会做出正确的选择，我将学着堆一个史上最好的雪人。"

The Snowman

It was late on a snowy Saturday afternoon. A young boy and his father were cleaning up the remaining leaves and branches that had fallen during the windy approach of the snowstorm. They stopped for a moment and sat quietly watching the snow fall.

Both were bundled up from head to toe. Mom insisted, "I'm the one who will have to take care of you if you catch a cold." So they complied, adding a scarf and hat as they walked out the door.

"Dad, my friend told me that every snowflake is different," the child said.

"I believe that's true," his dad replied.

There was silence.

"How do we know that?" The child asked.

Dad, now smiling, turned toward his son and said, "We just do."

"But they look all the same to me," the child added.

Now Dad felt obligated to come up with a more satisfying answer, one so profound that his son would remember this moment for years to come.

"Son, snowflakes are like people. God makes everyone of us different. We are each unique in a very special way. How do we know that? We just do." Not a good answer at all, he realized. It falls into that category of "Because I said so". "We can test it right now," he added.

The child stood up, put out his hand, and watched as snowflakes landed on his glove. "They ARE different," the boy said, "like people." Then came the big question. "When they are all together, they are so beautiful," he said, "then why don't they get along?"

"The snowflakes?" Dad asked.

"No, people, Dad. Why don't people get along? If people are like snowflakes, and each one is unique and special like you said, why don't they get along?"

Wow, that's a good question, one deserving a good answer.

"I mean, when you look at these snowflakes on my glove, they are all different. When you look at the snow in the yard, all together, they look the same. Together they are even more beautiful."

Dad sat there for a moment, thinking. "Choice." he said.

"Choice?" The child asked.

"One of the greatest gifts that God has given us is the gift of choice. As different as we all are, we have one thing in common. We can choose what we do, how we dress, where we live, and how we treat each other."

"So choice is a bad thing?" The boy asked.

"Oh, no. Only when we choose the wrong things."

"How do we know what's right and what's wrong?" The child asked.

Dad looked around, now, struggling to build upon this moment. Yes, it would have been easy to fall back on "We just do." But he was in a special place right now. He was given the chance to build upon the very foundation of his son's faith. Dad nervously shuffled his foot in the snow as he searched his heart for just the right answer.

"Let's say all of this snow is all the people of the world. Together they are beautiful. They are now given the gift of choice. They realize how well they work together, so they begin to build."

Dad reached down and divided the snow into two sides.

"Both sides acknowledge their differences. One says, Let's get together and build upon those differences. Let's do things that will help the world. The other side says the same thing, but can't come to an agreement on how to do it, so they each break off into separate piles."

Dad stopped for a moment and looked at his son. "Do you understand so far?"

"Yes, I think so," the boy replied.

Then, without saying another word, Dad continued to work with the snow. On the first side he built three large snowballs. On the other he made several smaller ones.

"Which side did the right thing?" He asked the boy.

The child looked at both sides but couldn't come up with an answer. "Dad, I don't know."

Then Dad placed the three larger snowballs on top of each other.

"It's a snowman!" The boy shouted.

"Now, which side did the right thing?"

"The side that made the snowman!" He replied with enthusiasm.

"Yes, all these people came together, recognizing how special each of them were. So they joined in an effort to build up mankind," Dad said.

The child then stood up and gathered an armful of the smaller snowballs. One by one he began to throw them at the other small pile of snow.

"What are you doing?" Dad asked.

"This is what happens when people can't work together, they have a war," he said.

Dad was stunned. He stood up, lifted the boy and held him tightly. Whispering in his ear, he said, "I pray to God that your world will learn to work and live together."

The boy leaned back in the comfort and protection of his father's arms, looked at him and said, "I will make the right choice. I will learn to build the best snowman ever."

有症状的乘客

[英国]伊夫林·沃

当詹姆斯先生关上他身后的侧门时,收音机的音乐声从他家的每扇窗户里传出来。艾格尼丝在厨房里,调到了一个电台。他的妻子在浴室里洗头,调到了另一个电台。

他听着比赛节目来到车库,进入车道。

他要开十二英里的车去车站,前五英里他一直心情不好。

他在大多数事情上是一个温和的人——可以说,除了一件事以外,在所有的事情上他都是一个温和的人:他憎恶无线电收音机。

无线电收音机不仅没有给他带来快乐,相反,给他带来了活生生的痛苦。多年以后,他开始认为这个发明是故意针对他自己的,是他的敌人的阴谋,他们想要扰乱他平静的晚年生活,让他痛苦。

他还远远谈不上是一个老人。事实上,他才五十五岁。他年纪轻轻就退休了,几乎是突如其来的,因为一笔小小的遗产使他的退休成为可能。他一生都喜欢安静。

詹姆斯太太没有与他共享这份偏好。

现在他们住在一所乡村小房子里,离一家合适的电影院有十二英里远。

对詹姆斯太太来说，无线电收音机是与干净的人行道和明亮的商店橱窗之间的纽带，是与千千万万同类的交流。

詹姆斯先生也是这么看的。他最在意的是侵犯他的隐私。他对女人这类物种的粗俗行为越来越反感。

就在这种心情下，他看见一个和他年龄相仿、身材魁梧的男人在路边向他示意让他搭车。他停了下来。

"我不知道你是否碰巧要去火车站？"那人彬彬有礼，说话的声音低沉而忧郁。

"是的。我得取一个包裹。上车吧。"

"你真是太好了！"

那人坐在詹姆斯先生旁边。他的靴子上满是灰尘，他瘫倒在座位上，好像是从很远的地方来的，很疲倦。他的一双手大而丑陋，灰白的头发剪得很短，一张瘦骨嶙峋的脸，两腮塌陷。

车开了大约一英里，他都没吭声。然后他突然问道："这辆车有无线电收音机吗？"

"当然没有。"

"那个把手是干什么用的？"他开始检查仪表盘。"这个呢？"

"一个是自动启动装置，另一个应该是点烟的。不能用了。"他严厉地继续说，"如果你让我停下来，希望听无线电的话，我只能建议先把你放下，让你在别人身上碰碰运气。"

"但愿不会。"他的乘客说。"我讨厌这东西。"

"我也是。"

"先生，你是万里挑一的人。我非常荣幸能认识你。"

"谢谢。这是一项残忍的发明。"

乘客的眼睛里闪烁着热情的同情。"这更糟。这是恶魔。"

"非常正确。"

"简直就是恶魔。它是魔鬼放在这里来毁灭我们的。你知道它传播最可怕的疾病吗?"

"我不知道。但我对此深信不疑。"

"它会导致癌症、肺结核、小儿麻痹症和普通感冒。我已经证明了这一点。"

"它肯定会引起头痛。"詹姆斯说。

"没有人比我头痛得更厉害。"他的乘客说。

"他们想让我头痛而死。但我太聪明了。你知道BBC有自己的秘密警察、自己的监狱、自己的刑讯室吗?"

"我早就怀疑了。"

"我知道,我都体验过。现在复仇的时候到了。"

詹姆斯先生不安地瞥了一眼他的乘客,把车开快了一点儿。

"我有一个计划。"大块头男人继续说。"我要到伦敦去执行这个计划,我要杀了局长,我要把他们全部杀光。"

他们默默地继续赶路。他们快到城郊时,一辆由一个女孩驾驶的大轿车与他们并驾齐驱,然后超过了他们。从里面传来了爵士乐队的声音,不会有错。大个子男人从座位上坐了起来,僵硬得像一个指针。

"你听见了吗?"他说。"她有一个无线电收音机。跟上她,快。"

"不行。"詹姆斯先生说。"我们永远追不上那辆车。"

"我们可以试一试。我们要试试,除非,"他用一种新的、更邪恶的语调说,"除非你不愿意。"

詹姆斯加速。但是那辆大轿车几乎看不见了。

他的乘客说:"以前有一次,我被骗了。英国广播公司派出了他们的一名间谍。他很像你。他假装是我的一个追随者。他说他要带我去总干事办公室。结果恰恰相反,他把我送进了监狱。现在我知道怎么对付间谍了。我把他们杀掉。"他向詹姆斯先生靠过去。

"我向你保证,亲爱的先生,你没有比我更忠实的支持者了。这只是一个汽车性能的问题。我不可能追上她。不过毫无疑问,我们会在车站找到她的。"

"我们会看到的。如果我们不这样做,我就知道该感谢谁,该怎样感谢他了。"

他们现在在城里,正朝车站走去。詹姆斯先生绝望地看着值勤的警察,但有人漫不经心地挥了挥手。在车站的院子里,旅客急切地东张西望。

"我没有看到那辆车。"他说。

詹姆斯先生摸索了一会儿,找到了门闩,然后滚了出去。"救命!"他大声呼救。"救命!这儿有个疯子。"

那人暴跳如雷,大喊一声,绕过车前,向他冲去。

就在这时,三个穿制服的人从车站门口冲了出来。一阵短暂的扭打,然后,他们熟练地把他们的人绑起来。

"我们原以为他会上火车的。"他们的头儿说。"你一定是把车开得惊心动魄,先生。"

詹姆斯先生几乎说不出话来。"无线电收音机。"他虚弱地低声说。

"哦,他一直在跟你说这件事,是吗?那你能来告诉我们真是太幸运了。你可能会说,这是他的小怪癖。我但愿你当时没有反驳他。"

"没有。"詹姆斯先生说。"至少一开始没有。"

"嗯,你比有些人幸运。他是不可以被激惹的,跟无线电收音机倒是无关。他会变得非常狂野。他上次逃跑时杀了两个人,第三个人也只剩半条命了。嗯,非常感谢您把他这么顺利地带进来,先生。我们一定要把他送回家。"

回家，詹姆斯先生沿着熟悉的路开回去。

"咦，"他刚一进屋，他的妻子就说，"你跑得好快。包裹在哪里？"

"我想我一定是忘了。"

"这可真不像你呀。哟，你看上去病得很厉害。我去叫艾格尼丝把无线电收音机关掉，你进来，她不可能听见。"

"不要。"詹姆斯先生说着，重重地坐了下来。"不要关掉无线电收音机，我喜欢，温馨如家。"

The Sympathetic Passenger

By Evelyn Waugh

As Mr. James shut the side door behind him, radio music burst from every window of his house. Agnes, in the kitchen, was tuned in to one station; his wife, washing her hair in the bathroom, to another.

The competing programmes followed him to the garage and into the lane.

He had twelve miles to drive to the station, and for the first five of them he remained in a black mood.

He was in most matters a mild-tempered person—in all matters, it might be said, except one: he abominated the wireless.

It was not merely that it gave him no pleasure; it gave active pain, and, in the course of years, he had come to regard the invention as being directed deliberately against himself, a conspiracy of his enemies to disturb and embitter what should have been the placid last years of his life.

He was far from being an old man; he was, in fact, in his

middle fifties; he had retired young, almost precipitously, as soon as a small legacy had made it possible. He had been a lover of quiet all his life.

Mrs. James did not share this preference.

Now they were settled in a small country house, twelve miles from a suitable cinema.

The wireless, for Mrs. James, was a link with the clean pavements and bright shop windows, a communion with millions of fellow beings.

Mr. James saw it in just that light, too. It was what he minded most—the violation of his privacy. He brooded with growing resentment on the vulgarity of womankind.

In this mood he observed a burly man of about his own age signalling to him for a lift from the side of the road. He stopped.

"I wonder if by any chance you are going to the railway station?" The man spoke politely with a low, rather melancholy voice.

"I am. I have to pick up a parcel. Jump in."

"That's very kind of you."

The man took his place beside Mr. James. His boots were dusty, and he sank back in his seat as though he had come from far and was weary. He had very large, ugly hands, close-cut grey hair, a bony, rather sunken face.

For a mile or so he did not speak. Then he asked suddenly, "Has this car got a wireless?"

"Certainly not."

"What is that knob for?" He began examining the dashboard. "And that?"

"One is the self-starter. The other is supposed to light cigarettes. It does not work. If," he continued sharply, "you have stopped me in the hope of hearing the wireless, I can only suggest that I put you down and let you try your luck on someone else."

"Heaven forbid," said his passenger, "I detest the thing."

"So do I."

"Sir, you are one among millions. I regard myself as highly privileged in making your acquaintance."

"Thank you. It is a beastly invention."

The passenger's eyes glowed with passionate sympathy. "It is worse. It is diabolical."

"Very true."

"Literally diabolical. It is put here by the devil to destroy us. Did you know that it spread the most terrible diseases?"

"I didn't know. But I can well believe it."

"It causes cancer, tuberculosis, infantile paralysis, and the common cold. I have proved it."

"It certainly causes headaches," said Mr. James.

"No man," said his passenger, "has suffered more excruciating headaches than I."

"They have tried to kill me with headaches. But I was too clever for them. Did you know that the BBC has its own secret police, its own prisons, its own torture chambers?"

"I have long suspected it."

"I know. I have experienced them. Now it is the time of revenge."

Mr. James glanced rather uneasily at his passenger and drove a little faster.

"I have a plan," continued the big man. "I am going to London to put it into execution. I am going to kill the Director-General. I shall kill them all."

They drove on in silence. They were nearing the outskirts of the town when a larger car driven by a girl drew abreast of them and passed. From inside it came the unmistakable sounds of a jazz band. The big man sat up in his seat, rigid as a pointer.

"Do you hear that?" He said. "She's got one. After her, quick."

"No good," said Mr. James. "We can never catch that car."

"We can try. We shall try, unless," he said with a new and more sinister note in his voice, "unless you don't want to."

Mr. James accelerated. But the large car was nearly out of sight.

"Once before," said his passenger, "I was tricked. The BBC sent one of their spies. He was very like you. He pretended to be one of my followers. He said he was taking me to the Director-

General's office. Instead he took me to a prison. Now I know what to do with spies. I kill them." He leaned towards Mr. James.

"I assure you, my dear sir, you have no more loyal supporter than myself. It is simply a question of cars. I cannot overtake her. But no doubt we shall find her at the station."

"We shall see. If we do not, I shall know whom to thank, and how to thank him."

They were in the town now and making for the station. Mr. James looked despairingly at the policeman on point duty, but was signalled on with a negligent flick of the hand. In the station yard the passenger looked round eagerly.

"I do not see that car," he said.

Mr. James fumbled for a second with the catch of the door and then tumbled out. "Help!" He cried. "Help! There's a madman here."

With a great shout of anger the man dodged round the front of the car and bore down on him.

At that moment three men in uniforms charged out of the station doorway. There was a brief scuffle, then, adroitly, they had their man strapped up.

"We thought he'd make for the railway," said their chief. "You must have had quite an exciting drive, sir."

Mr. James could scarcely speak. "Wireless," he muttered weakly.

"Ho, he's been talking to you about that, has he? Then you're very lucky to be here to tell us. It's his foible, as you might say. I hope you didn't disagree with him."

"No," said Mr. James. "At least, not at first."

"Well, you're luckier than some. He can't be crossed, not about wireless. Gets very wild. Why, he killed two people and half killed a third last time he got away. Well, many thanks for bringing him in so nicely, sir. We must be getting him home."

Home. Mr. James drove back along the familiar road.

"Why," said his wife when he entered the house. "How quick you've been. Where's the parcel?"

"I think I must have forgotten it."

"How very unlike you. Why, you're looking quite ill. I'll run in and tell Agnes to switch off the radio. She can't have heard you come in."

"No," said Mr. James, sitting down heavily. "Not switch off radio. Like it. Homely."

化敌为友

我已经有几个月没和她说话了,我现在甚至不记得是因为什么了。也许是因为我嫉妒。毕竟,一个女孩想要的一切,她似乎都拥有。她是班上最擅长各种体育运动的人。每一场比赛她都会赢,每一个球她都抓得住,并且每一个目标都能实现。她性格开朗,思维敏捷,善于言辞。事实上,除了我之外,没有一个人能够抵抗她的魅力。

我过去也很佩服她,至少在她证明自己可以画得更好、跑得更快、其他科目的分数更高之前如此。以前全班同学总是对我的画赞叹不已,但现在他们完全忽略了我的存在。我现在一无所长了。我也有点听之任之了。

我的父母也帮不上什么忙。"加油,汉娜,我们知道你可以做得更好。以萨曼莎为榜样,她难道不是一个很棒的女孩吗?你哪天可以邀请她到家里来。"

刚放暑假时,我觉得自己自由了。我的家人会像我们惯常的那样去湖边野营。只有这一次,我妈妈宣布了一些非常不受欢迎的消息。

"汉娜!你猜怎么着?我邀请了麦卡锡来参加我们的野营旅行。我和爸爸可以和麦卡锡夫妇、保罗、赖安、乔西(我的兄弟)一起出去玩,你可以和孩子们一起出去玩。这听起来怎么样?"

"糟透了。"我不高兴地低声说。

"我真的不知道你跟萨曼莎有什么过节。"妈妈皱着眉头答道。

然而,我不得不接受和处理这个状况,因为妈妈并没有改变主意的意思。

我知道萨曼莎和我根本就合不来。虽然我曾经喜欢过她,我们也依然不是天生的好朋友。我有一段时间不喜欢运动。我更喜欢花时间画画、画油画、弹钢琴、写作等。你明白的,就是艺术。

我唯一擅长的运动就是跑步。在她来之前,我每个学年都会参加田径比赛。而她的到来,好像把我的能量吸走了。现在,我在学校的比赛中只能得第四名或第五名。

在湖边,当麦卡锡家搭起帐篷时,我们全家住进了小屋。

我花了一周的时间回避萨曼莎,我一直待在小屋里看书,我拒绝了每一次徒步旅行、皮划艇以及与她相关的一切邀请。

我想我可以不跟她搭话地全身而退,但事实并非如此。

在我们旅行的第四天晚上,一场雷雨袭来。麦卡锡夫妇决定在我们的小屋里过夜,因为他们在他们带来的帐篷里感到不安全。当然,我必须和萨曼莎共用一个房间。我不知道我是怎么睡着的,但我确实睡着了。

深夜,我又醒了。暴风雨越来越大。我很热,急需使用厕所,我们的小屋里没有。所以我们不得不用一个不远处的户外厕所。

我跳下床,穿上一双袜子和鞋子,小心地不吵醒别人。可是,当我伸手去拿手电筒时,不小心踩到了萨曼莎的胳膊。

她马上醒了过来。

"你要去哪儿?"她坐了起来。

"去洗手间。"我答道,咬紧牙关。

"一个人去?!"她喊道。"我和你一起去。请稍等。"

"谢谢，不过我不会有事的。"我告诉她。

然而，她坚持要去，穿上了鞋子和夹克。

外面雨下得很大。闪电划过天空，雷声很大，好像小屋都跟着摇晃起来。隆隆的雷声和闪电之间的间隔很短，表明暴风雨就要来了。

我把夹克裹紧了些，开始朝外屋走去。

就在迈进户外厕所之前，我听到一声很大的断裂声，接着附近传来一声巨响。我当时没想太多。我只需要上厕所。

在回家的路上，我想着脱掉湿漉漉的夹克，爬到温暖舒适的床上。然而，当我们绕过小屋的拐角时，我立刻发现这是不可能的。

一棵大树横在小屋的入口处，挡住了门。无路可走，进不了门了。

萨曼莎也看到了。"哦，天哪！我们该怎么办？"她大声喊道。

我不假思索地问道："你的帐篷还在吗？"

"我想还在。"她回答。

"那我们就在那儿过夜，早上再找人帮忙。"我告诉她。

帐篷还是干的，但天气很冷，麦卡锡家的人把帐篷里他们所有的睡袋都拿走了。

然而，萨曼莎却有办法。她从剩下的许多袋子中的其中一个袋子里拿出一条野餐毯子，把它铺在两个泡沫上。

"这些不够，但是如果我们在一起用体温取暖，我们就不会冷了。"她说道。

首先我不得不和她在同一个班，然后我又不得已和她一起度假，再然后我非得和她合住一个房间，而现在我还要不得已和她共用一张床？！

为什么接二连三的状况都让我摊上了？

我别无选择，只能忍受，我们就是这样挨过这场暴风雨的。

清晨伴随着一项使命而来。寻求帮助。

我们穿上湿透了的鞋,直奔小屋。首先,我们要看看门那儿有没有我们没发现的可以通过的地方,再检查窗户和墙壁等有没有我们可以通过的地方。与此同时,我们计划让家人注意到我们,这样我们就可以告诉他们我们安好但需要帮助。我们也要确认他们是否也安好。

我们总是以这样或者那样的方式共事,被强行绑定在一起。我还是不喜欢她,但既然她是我唯一的伙伴,我也就接受下来。我想这可能与我想证实我的能力有关,我想向萨曼莎证明我能救出我的家人,至少能协助救出我的家人,也许这样我们就能打个平手了。

"窗户太小,人过不去!"萨曼莎对我大声喊道。"不过这扇窗户的玻璃碎了,我想我们可以通过这里跟家人沟通。"

这扇窗户距离门很近。

"门被彻底封住了。"我很肯定地说。

我们下一步就是要引起他们的注意。我们踮着脚尖儿站在窗前,喊着父母。

萨曼莎的哥哥德克兰先过来了,接着是我的哥哥保罗。

"谢天谢地,你们都安好!"德克兰喊道。

"是啊,我们到处找你们,猜测你们出去了。我们都为你们担心。"保罗补充道。

"我们要去寻求帮助。告诉爸爸妈妈我们安好。"我对他们说。

说完,我和萨姆①沿着这条路走了下去。这里的电话设施坏了,我们也都没有电话,所以这条路走不通。不过,如果我们能找到也在湖边野营的人,我们就可以请他们把我们载到附近的萨洛弗兰克城,我们在

---

① 萨姆(Sam)是萨曼莎的小称。

那里就可以得到帮助了。

我们跑了大约五分钟，才意识到这条路距离湖越来越远了。

我们现在面临两个选择：走回头路，按照原计划行动；改变我们原来的计划，继续沿着这条路走，看看路边会不会有人家。

"嗯，我说走下去吧，只要我们沿着这条路走下去，我们就会到达某个地方。可是，我们在湖边能不能找到人就不一定了。"萨曼莎建议。

我不赞同她的提议，于是反驳道："可是，我们并不知道要走多久才能看到人家。如果我们继续沿着这条路走下去，可能要走几个小时。如果路上的岔路很多，要回去就更困难了。而沿着湖边走的话，就仅限于湖边，回去就不会迷路。"

我们就这样争论着，我们可能是一边走一边争论的。

是她先注意到了这个问题。"我让步，我们就沿着湖边走。我们在这里浪费时间，我们的家人还困在那间小屋里，等我们去营救呢。"

"我们沿着这条路走。"我回答。"我现在同意你的意见了。"

"我觉得沿着湖边走挺好的。"

"我觉得沿着这条路走也挺好的。"我都不知道我为什么先开那个口。

我们交换了一下眼神，不约而同地瘫在地上哈哈大笑起来。

"我们做好朋友吧。"她提议。

萨曼莎要跟我做好朋友？我以前以为她一直是鄙视我的，而这么长时间以来原来她竟然一直想做我的好朋友？！

我最终意识到我也想做她的好朋友。原来是我错看了她。

于是，我们选择了继续沿着这条路走下去，我们开始手挽着手一起向前走。

半小时以后,我们看到了一幢房子,我们的肚子也咕噜咕噜地叫起来,而我们靠说话和跑步来分散注意力。我们有任务要完成,我们一定要完成任务。

"跟你赛跑!"萨曼莎喊道。

"各就各位,预备,跑!"

就在我们开始冲刺的那一刻,我意识到输赢都不重要。可能我跟萨曼莎并没有那么多共同之处,可是,人们往往由于彼此不同而相互吸引。

此外,我们有共同的经历,营救两家人无疑是一项壮举,而得到一个朋友更了不起。

我猜测最坏的敌人已经化为最好的朋友。

Worst Enemy-Best Friends

I hadn't spoken with her in months. I don't even remember why now. Perhaps it was because I was jealous. After all, she seems to have everything a girl could want. She's the best in the class at anything sport related. She wins every race, catches every ball, and makes every goal. She's outgoing, quick witted and has a way with words. In fact there isn't a soul I know who can resist her charm—except me that is.

I used to admire her, too. Until she proved that she could draw better, run faster, and score higher in every other subject. The class used to ooh and ah over my drawings, but now they ignore me completely. I'm not good at anything anymore. I sort of just gave up trying.

My parents don't help either. "Come on Hanna, we know you can do better. Take Samantha for example. Isn't she a great girl? You should invite her over someday."

I thought that I was free when the summer holidays started. My family was going to go camping at the lake like we always do. Only this time, my mom announced some very unwelcome news.

"Hanna! Guess what? I've invited the McCarthy's on our camping trip. Dad and I can hang out with Mr. and Mrs. McCarthy, and Paul, Ryan, Josh (my brothers) and you can hang out with the kids. How does that sound?"

"Terrible," I groaned.

"I honestly don't get what you have against Samantha," my mom frowned.

However, I just had to suck it up and deal with it. My mom wasn't changing her mind.

I knew that Samantha and I wouldn't get along at all. Even if I had liked her, we just weren't made for each other. I wasn't sportsy, period. I preferred to spend my time drawing, painting, playing piano, writing, etc . You know, the arts.

The only sport I was any good at was running. I had made it to track and field every school year until she came. It was as if she had sucked away my energy. Now I only came in fourth or fifth in the school races compared to my normal firsts.

At the lake, my family organized themselves in the cabin while the McCarthy's set up their tent.

I spent the week ignoring Samantha and staying inside reading. I turned down each invitation of hiking, kayaking and everything else that had to do with her.

I thought I could get away without talking to her, but it wasn't so.

On the fourth night of our trip, a thunderstorm struck. The McCarthy's decided to spend the night in our cabin because they didn't feel safe in the tent they had brought. I, of course, had to share a room with Samantha. I don't know how I managed to fall asleep, but I did.

I woke up late at night. The storm had gotten worse. I was hot and desperately needed to use the toilet, our cabin didn't have one, so we had to use an outhouse a short walk away.

I hopped out of bed and pulled on a pair of socks and shoes, being careful not to wake anyone up. However, when I was reaching for my flashlight, I accidentally stepped on Samantha's arm.

She woke up immediately.

"Where are you going?" She asked sitting up.

"To the bathroom." I replied, clenching my teeth.

"Alone?!" She exclaimed. "I'll go with you. Just a minute."

"Thanks, but I'll be fine," I told her.

However, she insisted and got on her shoes and jacket.

Outside, it was raining hard. Lightning flashed across the sky and the thunder was so loud it seemed to shake the cabin. The intervals between the rumbles of the thunder and the flashes of lightning were very short, a sign that the storm was quite close.

I pulled my jacket tighter and began towards the outhouse.

Just before stepping in, I heard a loud crack and then a quite nearby crash. I didn't think too much of it then. I just needed to go to the washroom.

On our way back, I thought of stripping off my soaking jacket and crawling into my nice warm bed. As we rounded the corner to the cabin however, I saw immediately that it wouldn't be possible.

A big tree lay across the entrance of the cabin, blocking the door. There was no way to get back in.

Samantha saw it, too. "Oh my gosh! What should we do?" She exclaimed.

Thinking fast, I asked, "Is your tent still okay?"

"I think so," she answered.

"Then we'll spend the night there and get help in the morning," I told her.

The tent was still dry, but it was super cold and the MaCarthy's had taken all of their sleeping bags inside.

Samantha, however, knew what to do. She pulled out a picnic blanket from one of the many bags left behind and spread it out over two foams.

"It's not a lot, but if we use each others body-heat, we'll be warm enough." She said.

First I had to be in the same class as her, then I needed to spend a vacation with her, then I had to share a room with her. Now I had to share a bed with her?!

Why did this have to happen to me?

I had no choice but to go through with it and that's how we got through the storm.

Morning dawned on us with a mission. Get help.

We pulled on our soaked shoes, and made our way to the cabin. We would first see if the door was accessible by some way we hadn't seen, and check windows, walls etc. At the same time, we planned to try to get our families attention so that we could communicate that we were okay and were going to get help. We would make sure that they were okay as well.

Somehow, being forced to work together had bound us in a way. I still didn't like her, but if she was going to be the only company I could get, then I would take it. I suppose that it maybe had to do with the fact that this was something I could do. I would prove to Samantha that I could save our families, or at least help to save our families, and maybe we would be even then.

"The windows are too small for anyone to get through!" Samantha called to me. "I think we'll be able to communicate through this one though. It's been broken for us."

It was one of the windows near the door.

"The door is completely blocked." I affirmed.

Our next step was to get their attention. We stood at the window on our tippy-toes and hollered for our parents.

It was Samantha's brother, Declan, who came over first, followed by my brother, Paul.

"Thank goodness you guys are okay!" Declan exclaimed.

"Yeah, we were looking for you everywhere, and figured you had gone outside. We were worried about you." Paul added.

"We're going to get help. Just tell Mom and Dad we're okay." I told them.

At that, Sam and I took off down the road. Phone service was bad here, and neither of us had phones anyway, so that option was closed. However, if we could find somebody else who was camping along the lake, we could get them to drive us to the nearby town of Salofrank. We would get help there.

We ran for about five minutes, before realizing that the road was taking us away from the lake.

Now we were faced with two options. Go back, and follow the lake according to plan, or change our plans, and hope for a house along this road.

"Well I say go on. At least if we follow the road, we know we'll be getting somewhere. We don't know if we'll find anybody along the lake." Samantha proposed.

I didn't want to agree with her, so I argued against it. "We don't know how long it is until the next house though. If we just keep following the road, it might take us hours. It'll be harder to trace our steps if there are multiple forks in the road, whereas along the lake, we just walk along the lake."

And so we argued. We probably argued for just as long as we

had been walking.

She noticed it first. "We'll just go along the lake. I give in. While we waste our time, our families are stuck in that cabin, relying on us to get them out."

"We'll go by the road," I countered. "I agree with you now."

"I'm fine with going by the lake."

"The road's fine, too." I don't see why I opened my mouth in the first place.

We exchanged glances and collapsed on the ground laughing.

"Let's just be friends," she said.

Samantha wanted to be my friend? I thought that she looked down on me and this whole time she actually wanted to be my friend?!

I finally realized that I wanted to be friends, too. I had misjudged her.

So we chose the road and arm in arm, we started to walk.

Half and hour later, we spotted a house. Our stomachs were growling, but we distracted ourselves by talking and running. We had a mission to fulfill, and we would fulfill it.

"Race you!" Samantha called.

"On your mark, get set, GO!"

As we started to sprint, I realized that it didn't matter if I won or not. Maybe Samantha and I didn't have much in common, but often it's because people are the opposite of the other that they are attracted to one another.

Besides, we had this experience to share. Saving two families was a great accomplishment for sure, but gaining a friend was even greater.

I guess that worst enemies make the best friends.

不要告诉我我很漂亮

[英国] 南希·米切尔

我到底是什么时候意识到自己丑的,我不记得了。上六年级的时候,我把自信放错了位置,我自查之后,把自己框进"苗条"和"金发"的类型,深信自己起码还属于过得去的有吸引力的类型。上七年级的时候,我如梦方醒,可能是在一个同班同学的帮助下。人都知道,初中生是最促狭的。

那段时间我情绪低落。可是,我的内心还抱有希望,希望到了高中会峰回路转。以对《斯威特瓦利高中》和《十七岁》杂志的细读为依据,这似乎是合情合理的。可是,在初中和高中之间的那个假期,我以为我的外貌有了改善,等我上了高中一年级,我再一次陷入了绝望。我的新同学个个身材高挑,皮肤晒成了棕褐色,看起来像小大人。而我呢?还是那么丑。

我心烦意乱地回了家。我妈妈感觉到了,问我出了什么问题。"没人愿意做我的朋友,"我告诉她,"我不好看。"

"哦,南希,"我妈妈说,"你当然很漂亮。我觉得你很漂亮。"

我哭是因为我知道这不是真的。或者更确切地说,因为这是真的——我妈妈当然认为我很漂亮——但我想让其他人认为我很漂亮,因为十四岁的我意识到了一个残酷的现实：当你还是一个女孩的时候，其他人认为你是不是很漂亮，这很重要。这几乎就是一切。

现在，我希望时光倒流，对当年十四岁的我说："不是你看起来像什么决定了你是什么样的人，而是你做什么决定了你是什么样的人。"

因为对于漂亮这个问题你几乎无能为力，尤其是你在十四岁的时候，你既迟钝又笨拙，皮肤油腻。但是你可以改变你所做的事情。你随时都可以改变。

我想起了我花在镜子前的时间，希望我的青春痘能消失。希望我的屁股小些，因为尽管我体重距离标准体重还差十五磅，我还是觉得自己很胖。我母亲说的是真的，尽管我不想听她说话，而且在这几年的时间里，我已经明白了这一点。青春痘只是暂时性的，我认为是缺点的东西在对的人眼里变成了财富。漂亮并非只有一种样态。

认识到这一点对我而言是巨大的解脱，真希望这不是真的。我恨自己浪费了时间和精力来希望自己变得更漂亮，那些时间我应该用来跟家人在一起，或骑自行车、拉中提琴、给朋友写有趣的便条，蜷缩在地图册上记一记非洲海岸上的种种。可当时我在《十七岁》《斯威特瓦利高中》上看到的、在教会的青年小组的男孩子那里听到的，都是同样的话："你只要漂亮就行。"只有漂亮才会有人注意你。我信了他们，因为人们都是那么想的，但这是一个谎言，我现在意识到了，我恨这个谎言。

如果我现在有个小女儿，我想对她说："你很善良。你很聪明，你很重要。你跟人家说的话重要，你对待别人的方式重要，你的话有治愈的力量，也有伤害人的力量，你要明智地使用这些力量。你要爱别人，爱学习。"我有时还要告诉她，她很漂亮，但不能让漂亮来定义她，也许她会生活在真实的世界里。

有时候，跟我一起出去约会的男人会说我漂亮。前几次听了感觉还不错，但听多了就会觉得是老生常谈，很难感到心满意足。我想，你们就不能说些更悦耳的话？若有人经常告诉一个男人他有多漂亮，男人也很难心满意足。我想知道，你们认为我是可爱的，不过，你们认为我还有其他优点吗？告诉我，我能让你们开怀大笑，你们爱我的创造力，爱我的理想。告诉我，除了我，没有谁让你这么快乐过。

但不要告诉我，我很漂亮。

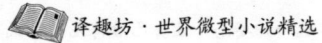

Don't Tell Me I'm Beautiful

By Nancy Mitchell

I can't remember exactly when it was I realized I was ugly. A misplaced sort of confidence carried me through sixth grade, a conviction that since I checked the boxes of "skinny" and "blonde", I must be at least passably attractive. I was probably disabused of this sometime in the seventh grade, probably with the help of one of my classmates. Junior high kids are the worst people known to man.

That was a low time. But still, I cherished the hope that by the time I got to high school, this would all turn around. This seemed reasonable, based on close readings of Sweet Valley High and Seventeen magazine. But after the summer between junior high and high school, during which I imagined I had improved, I went to freshman orientation and was plunged back into despair. There were all my new classmates, long and tan and looking like little adults. And me? Still ugly.

I came home distraught. My mother sensed this, and asked me

what was wrong. "Nobody wants to be my friend," I told her. "I'm not pretty."

"Oh, Nancy," my mother said, "of course you're pretty. I think you're beautiful."

I cried because I knew it wasn't true. Or rather, because it was true—of course my mother thought I was beautiful—but I wanted other people to think I was beautiful, because at 14 I had latched onto a cruel reality: When you're a girl, whether or not other people think you are pretty means a lot. It is almost everything.

Here's what I wish I could go back in time and say to 14-year-old me: "You are not what you look like. You are what you do."

Because there is very little you can do about how pretty you are. Especially when you're 14 and gawky and awkward and have greasy skin. But you can change what you do. You can change that all the time.

I think about the time I spent looking in the mirror, wishing my zits would go away. Wishing my butt were smaller, because even though I was 15 pounds underweight, I somehow thought I was fat. What my mother said was true, even though I didn't want to listen to her, and the intervening years have made that clear to me. Zits are only temporary, and the things I thought were flaws have turned out to be assets to the right people. Pretty doesn't always look the same.

But I hate that this is such a huge relief to me. I hate the time and the mental energy I wasted, wishing and trying to be prettier, time that I could've spent with my family, or riding my bike, or playing the viola, or writing funny notes to my friends, or curled up with the atlas memorizing the coast of Africa. Everywhere, from Seventeen and from Sweet Valley High and from the boys in my church's youth group, I heard the same thing: You only matter if you're pretty. That's the only way you will get people to pay attention to you. And I believed them, because it was true, that was what everybody thought, but it was such a lie and I realize that now and I hate it.

If I have a little girl I want to say to her: You are kind. You are smart. You are important. The things you say to people matter. The way you treat people matters. In your words, you possess the power to heal and to harm. Use them wisely. Love people. Learn things. And I will tell her, sometimes, that she is beautiful, but I will remind her that this is not what defines her. Maybe she will live in a world where that is true.

Sometimes, men I go out with tell me that I'm pretty. It's nice the first few times, but it gets old after a while. Come up with something better, I think. No man would ever be satisfied with constantly being told how beautiful he was. I like to know that you think I am lovely, but do you think other things about me? Tell me that I'm smart, that I make you laugh, that you love my creativity, my ambition. Tell me that nobody else has ever made you this happy.

But don't tell me I'm beautiful.

应急预案

[美国] 杰夫 C. 吉布森

特工本杰明·特灵端着两杯咖啡走进审讯室，并把其中一杯放在犯罪嫌疑人查尔斯·亚瑟·格罗根面前的桌子上。

特灵说道："特工约翰逊告诉我你改变主意了。顺便说一句，我们正在录像。"他指了指天花板上的摄像头，"之后我们会做出正式声明。"

格罗根点了点头："所以，如果我配合，罪行就只是非法持有枪支，而不是抢劫银行？"

"对。你只要把你知道的关于夏莲娜·博蒙特的一切全告诉我们就行了。"

"成交。从哪里开始？"

"从头说起。"

"好。"他深吸了一口气。"夏莲娜·博蒙特是世界上最了不起的银行抢劫犯。真的，她是个天才。从来没有被抓住过，恐怕以后也不会。没有冒犯你的意思，不要见怪。"

"没关系。"

"每次抢劫她都计划周密、一丝不苟。无论发生什么事，她都能拿出应急预案。我知道的一切都是她教的。"

"认识她之前,你从来没有抢劫过银行吗?"

"没有,警官,从来没有。"他叹了口气,把目光移开。"我们在一起度过了美好的一年,非常愉快的一年。我们一起抢劫,在成堆的钞票上做爱,去最好的餐厅吃饭。这是我一生中最幸福的一年。"

"多么甜蜜。"特灵扫了一眼笔记。"你认识她时,她二十二岁?"

"是的。那时候她已经是老手了。是她的前男友,一个叫米奇的家伙教给她的。他告诉她,对于一个银行抢劫犯来说,最需要的不是大脑、胆量或纯粹的意志,而是纪律。如果你不遵守纪律,再好的计划也是屎。"

"是的。"

"她跟米奇抢劫了七次银行,能学的都学会了。但是她不得不甩掉他,因为大部分时间他都在吸毒,精神恍惚,对作案越来越马虎。不过真正让她愤怒的是他对她的忽视。像夏莲娜这样的女人,最受不了的就是这个。"

"稍后我们会去抓捕米奇。你一共抢劫了多少家银行?"

格罗根喝了一小口咖啡。"五家。前四家都堪称完美,一切都与她所计划的严丝合缝。第五家没那么完美了,否则我也不会在这里了。"

"出了什么问题?"

"离开银行时,我为夏莲娜撑着门,她把抢来的钱装在一个超大的手提包里,这时有个讨厌的顾客从地上弓身站起来,企图抓住我。我根本不该让他离我那么近。我的分工是控制普通市民、注意时间和街道上的情况,而夏莲娜的分工则是抢现金。他肯定是趁我转身时爬起来的。

"他一把把我的脸撞在门上。喏,你看。"格罗根指着额头上的绷带说。"我一胳膊肘打在他的太阳穴上,但他并没有倒下,于是我朝他头上方开了一枪。他明白了,当场就尿裤子了!"格罗根轻声笑着说。

特灵没笑："继续。"

"我出去的时候,夏莲娜正坐在方向盘后面准备加大油门,面具后面,她圆睁双目,眼神里全是愤怒。我匆忙坐进副驾驶,然后我们开车离去。过了几个街区之后,我才扯下面具,擦去眼睛里流出的血。"

"我们拐进一个零售店,把赃款藏在多用途箱里,然后——"

"等等,为什么藏在多用途箱里?"

"这是夏莲娜的主意。她一直在用多用途箱。一把标准的万能钥匙就能打开,而且里面的空间够大。"

特灵记了下来。"为什么要把钱都藏起来呢?为什么不逃之夭夭呢?"

格罗根喝了一大口咖啡。"这正是她的计划最漂亮的地方,我们把现金藏起来,然后坐等事件冷却。即使抓到我们,你们也不能立案。没有赃物,没有指纹,没有有效的身份验证,你们什么都没有。

"然后,我们又回到了汽车旅馆。我情况很糟,头伤得厉害,但是夏莲娜草草给我处理了一下,就说我会好的。然后她出门去烧我们刚才穿的衣服。她还拿走了我的手枪,因为与我刚才射出去的子弹匹配。

"我吃了几颗止痛药就睡下了。醒来时,夏莲娜已经回来了,还带了一些中国的外卖。外面一片昏暗。我的头还在疼,不过我觉得这是药物和酒精的缘故。我们又睡下了。

"第二天早上,她说我们必须得执行其中一个应急预案了,得马上离开这个城市。我的分工是去取抢来的钱,她的分工是把我们的行李拿到车站并负责买车票。还有三个小时,时间很宽裕。

"我赶到零售店后面的小胡同时,那里空无一人,于是我跑到多用途箱里一把拿起了大提包。这时胡同里突然警笛大作,灯火通明。我差点儿被吓出心脏病来。后面的事情你都知道了。"

特灵点了点头。"你看到我打开大提包,里面塞满了报纸,还有你在抢劫中使用的手枪。"

"是的。而且你们还收到了一个匿名举报,是一个女的举报的,对吗?"

"对。你从来没有怀疑过她会背叛你吗?"

"绝对没有!是的,我把事情搞砸了,但是没有什么是不能从头再来的。我们仍然可以一起逃之夭夭。我们曾相爱过。至少我爱过她。"他露出了痛苦的表情,把手里的杯子都捏瘪了。

"直到一个小时前,我才明白了这一切。当时我在楼下,被锁在椅子上。我环顾着四周,顾影自怜,就在这时我看到了一幅挂历,过去的日期都被划掉了。那时我才明白过来。"他只得咧嘴笑了笑。"夏莲娜的生日是三天前,我彻底给忘了,像夏莲娜这样的女人,最受不了的就是这个!"

Contingency Plan

By Jeff C. Gibson

Special Agent Benjamin Turling stepped into the interrogation room with two cups of coffee. He put one on the table in front of Charles Arthur Grogan, suspect.

Turling said, "Agent Johnson tells me you changed your mind. We're recording, by the way." He pointed to the camera in the ceiling. "We'll do a formal statement later."

Grogan nodded. "So if I cooperate, it's only the weapons charge? No bank robbery?"

"Correct. All you have to do is tell me everything you know about Sharlene Beaumont."

"Deal. Where do I start?"

"Try the beginning."

"Right." He took a deep breath. "Sharlene Beaumont is the greatest bank robber in the world. Seriously. She's a genius. Never got caught, and I doubt she ever will. No offence."

"None taken."

"She plans her jobs to the last detail. No matter what happens, she has a contingency plan. She taught me everything I know."

"You never robbed a bank before you met her?"

"No sir, never." Grogan sighed and looked away. "But we had a great year together. One glorious year. Pulling jobs, making love on piles of cash. The finest restaurants. It was the best year of my life."

"How sweet." Turling glanced at his notes. "She was twenty-two when you met her?"

"Right. She was already a pro by then. Her old boyfriend taught her how, a guy named Mitch. He told her that the most important thing a bank robber needed, more than brains or balls or sheer will, was discipline. The best plan in the world wasn't worth shit if you didn't follow it."

"True."

"She pulled seven jobs with Mitch and learned all she could. But she had to dump him. He was stoned most of the time, getting sloppy on the job. What really pissed her off was that he neglected her. You just don't do that to a woman like Sharlene."

"We'll get to Mitch later. How many banks did you rob?"

Grogan took a sip. "Five. The first four went down perfect, exactly like she said they would. The fifth, not so perfect. Otherwise I wouldn't be here."

"What happened?"

"We were leaving the bank and I was holding the door for Sharlene, who had the loot in an oversized purse, when some asshole customer lunged up off the floor and tried to tackle me. I never should have let him get that close. It was my job to control the civilians, and keep an eye on the clock and the street, while Sharlene grabbed the cash. He must have crept up while my back was turned.

"He slammed my face into the door. Gave me this." Grogan pointed to the bandage on his forehead. "I threw an elbow to his temple but he didn't go down. So I fired a shot over his head. He got the message, all right. He pissed his pants!" Grogan chuckled.

Turling didn't. "Go on."

"When I got outside, Sharlene was behind the wheel, gunning the engine, her eyes wild behind her mask. I slid into the passenger seat and we took off. I waited until we were a couple blocks away before tearing off my mask and wiping the blood from my eyes."

"We switched cars and went to the strip mall and stashed the loot in the utility box. Then we—"

"Wait a minute. Why a utility box?"

"It was Sharlene's idea. She uses them all the time. You can open them with a standard skeleton key and there's usually enough room inside."

Turling wrote that down. "Why hide the money at all? Why

not just run?"

Grogan took a gulp of his coffee. "That's the beauty of her plan. We stash the cash and let things cool off. Even if you track us down, you don't have a case. Without the loot or a fingerprint or a positive ID, you ain't got shit.

"Anyway, we went back to the motel room. I was in bad shape. My head was pounding but Sharlene patched me up and said I'd be fine. Then she left to torch the clothes we'd been wearing. She also took my pistol, since you could match it to the bullet I fired.

"I took a couple painkillers and crashed. When I woke up, Sharlene was back with some Chinese takeout. It was dark outside. I still had a headache but I think it was from the pills and booze. We went back to sleep.

"The next morning, she said we had to implement one of her contingency plans and leave town right away. It was my job to go get the loot while she took our luggage to the bus station and bought tickets. We had three hours. Plenty of time.

"When I got to the alley behind the strip mall, it was deserted, so I ran over to the utility box and grabbed the bag. Then the whole place exploded with sirens and lights. I almost had a heart attack. You know the rest."

Turling nodded. "You watched me open the bag. It was filled with newspapers. And the pistol you used in the robbery."

"Yeah. And you guys got an anonymous tip. From a woman, right?"

"Correct. You never suspected she might betray you?"

"Hell no! Sure, I fucked up, but nothing we couldn't recover from. We still could have escaped together. We were in love. I was, anyway." He grimaced and crumpled his cup.

"I didn't figure it out until an hour ago, when I was downstairs, chained to the bench. I was looking around and feeling sorry for myself when I saw a wall calendar with the old dates crossed off. That's when it hit me." He grinned, because he had to. "Sharlene's birthday was three days ago. I completely forgot. And you just don't do that to a woman like Sharlene!"

活　着

　　两个男人一前一后走得很慢，他们穿过河流的浅水区域。目光所及之处，只有石头和土，脚底的河水也冰凉刺骨。他们身上背着装毛毯的包，包里有枪却没子弹，有火柴却没食物。

　　后面那个男人突然被石头给绊倒了，脚伤严重，于是向前喊道："喂！比尔，我的脚受伤了。"比尔却头也没回，径直继续向前走。

　　这个男人就一个人被孤零零地留在这片空地上了，但他没有迷路。他记得回他们营地的路，他在那里能找到食物和子弹。于是，他挣扎着起来，一瘸一拐地向前走着。比尔肯定会在那儿等着他，然后他们一起向南前往哈德逊湾公司。他已经整整两天没有进食了，常常只是停下来摘一些小浆果塞进嘴里。这些浆果没有滋味，还吃不饱，可是他知道不吃不行。

　　晚上，他点个火堆，睡得像个死人。早上醒来以后，他从背包里取出一个小袋子。这个袋子重十五英镑，他不知道自己还能不能拿得动，但也不能扔下，只能随身带着。他把小袋子放回包里，抬起腿，继续蹒跚而行。

　　他脚上受的伤跟饥饿比起来反倒不算什么了，这驱使着他一直走到夜幕降临时分。毛毯已经湿了，但他只知道饿，整夜都睡不好，梦见盛宴和各种各样的食物。醒来以后，感觉很冷，身体也不舒服，这才发现自己迷路了,但那个小袋子还在身边。他挣扎着继续走,感觉袋子越来越沉,他打开装满小块黄金的袋子,把其中一半的金子倒在一块岩石上。

十一天过去了,天气寒冷、阴雨连绵的十一天。一天,他在路边发现了一具鹿的白骨,白骨上没有一丝肉。这个男人只能打碎骨头,像个野兽一样吮吸、咀嚼里面的骨髓。他明天也会变成一堆白骨吧?这有什么不可能的?这就是生命啊,只有活着生物才会受伤,死了就不会受伤了。死亡意味着长眠。为什么他不愿意死去呢?其实他也不想挣扎着活下去了,但他体内有一种生存的本能,不愿意就这样死去,这促使他继续前行。

一天早上,他在一条河边醒来,目光顺着河流缓缓向前,汇入一片发光的大海,当他看到海上有一艘船的时候,他就闭上了眼睛,因为他知道这块陆地上既没有海,也没有船,这些不过是幻觉。这时,他听到身后有动静,于是转过身来。原来是一只病弱的老狼,正在向他慢慢靠近。这不是幻觉,他想。这个男人回头望去,大海和那条船还在那里。他就不明白了,他是不是一直在北上,离营地越来越远,离大海越来越近了?他站起身,开始慢慢地向船走去,心里非常清楚那只病狼就跟在身后。下午,他在路边发现了一个人的尸骨,旁边还有一小袋金子,就像他的一样。原来比尔把金子一直带到了这儿,这下他就能把比尔的金子带上船了。哈哈哈哈!跟比尔相比,他笑到了最后。他的笑声听起来却像动物的低嚎一样,饿狼回应着他的嚎叫。男人突然停下转过身去,他怎么能对着比尔的骨头发出哈哈大笑,还带走他的金子呢?

男人这时已经病得很厉害了,他用手脚和膝盖爬着。他已经失去了一切——他的毛毯、他的枪,还有他的金子,只有这只饿狼一直尾随着他。最终他没有力气向前了,他倒下了。饿狼靠了过来,而男人早有了准备。他跃到饿狼背上，合上它的嘴，用尽最后的力气咬上去，狼血溅进嘴里，是对生存的渴望赋予了他足够的力气。他用牙咬着狼，咬死了它，然后仰面朝天倒在地上，昏睡过去了。

　　船上的人看见沙滩上有个奇怪的东西，以每小时大约二十英里的速度，正在朝他们挪动。这些人跑出船去看，几乎不敢相信那是一个人。

　　三个星期以后，男人感觉好些了，就向他们讲述了自己的经历。但有件事很奇怪——他总害怕船上的食物不够。船上的人发现这个男人越来越胖，于是减少了他的食物量，但他依然越来越胖。后来有一天，他们看见这个男人在衬衫下藏了很多面包，检查他的床铺，结果在毛毯下面也发现了食物。这下他们明白了。他们说，男人会慢慢地走出那个阴影的。

Love of Life

Two men walked slowly, one after the other, through the shallow water of a stream. All they could see were stones and earth. The stream ran cold over their feet. They had blanket packs on their backs. They had guns, but no bullets; matches, but no food.

Suddenly the man who followed fell over a stone. He hurt his foot badly and called: "Hey, Bill, I've hurt my foot." Bill continued straight on without looking back.

The man was alone in the empty land, but he was not lost. He knew the way to their camp, where he would find food and bullets. He struggled to his feet and limped on. Bill would be waiting for him there, and together they would go south to the Hudson Bay Company. He had not eaten for two days. Often he stopped to pick some small berries and put them into his mouth. The berries were tasteless, and did not satisfy, but he knew he must eat them.

In the evening he built a fire and slept like a dead man. When he woke up, the man took out a small sack. It weighed fifteen pounds. He wasn't sure if he could carry it any longer. But he couldn't leave it behind. He had to take it with him. He put it back into his pack, rose to his feet and staggered on.

His foot hurt, but it was nothing compared with his hunger, which made him go on until darkness fell. His blanket was wet, but he knew only that he was hungry. Through his restless sleep he dreamed of banquets and of food. The man woke up cold and sick, and found himself lost. But the small sack was still with him. As he dragged himself along, the sack became heavier and heavier. The man opened the sack, which was full of small pieces of gold. He left half the gold on a rock.

Eleven days passed, days of rain and cold. One day he found the bones of a deer. There was no meat on them. The man broke the bones and he sucked and chewed on them like an animal. Would he, too, be bones tomorrow? And why not? This was life. Only life hurt. There was no hurt in death. To die was to sleep. Then why was he not ready to die? He, as a man, no longer strove. It was the life in him, unwilling to die, that drove him on.

One morning he woke up beside a river. Slowly he followed it with his eyes and saw it emptying into a shining sea. When he saw a ship on the sea, he closed his eyes. He knew there could be no ship, no sea, in this land. A vision, he told himself. He heard a noise behind him, and turned around. A wolf, old and sick, was coming slowly toward him. This was real, he thought. The man turned back, but the sea and the ship were still there. He didn't understand. Had he been walking north, away from the camp, toward the sea? He stood up and started slowly toward the ship, knowing full well the sick wolf was following him. In the afternoon, he found some bones of a man. Beside the bones was a small sack of gold, like his own. So Bill had carried his gold to the end. He would carry Bill's gold to the ship. Ha——ha! He would have the last laugh on Bill. His laughing sounded like the low cry of an animal. The wolf cried back. The man stopped suddenly and turned away. How could he laugh about Bill's bones and take his gold?

The man was very sick now. He crawled about, on hands and knees. He had lost everything——his blanket, his gun, and his gold. Only the wolf stayed with him hour after hour. At last he could go on no further. He fell. The wolf came close to him, but the man was ready. He got on top of the wolf and held its mouth closed. Then he bit it with his last strength. The wolf's blood streamed into his mouth. Only love of life gave him enough strength. He held the wolf with his teeth and killed it, then he fell on his back and slept.

The men on the ship saw a strange object lying on the beach. It was moving toward them——perhaps twenty feet an hour. The men went over to look and could hardly believe it was a man.

Three weeks later, when the man felt better, he told them his story. But there was one strange thing——he seemed to be afraid that there wasn't enough food on the ship. The men also noticed that he was getting fat. They gave him less food, but still he grew fatter with each day. Then one day they saw him put a lot of bread under his shirt. They examined his bed and found food under his blanket. The men understood. He would recover from it, they said.

死如树脂

[西班牙]安东尼·佩罗塔

莱恩站在一旁,看着父亲准备把后院的一棵松树砍倒。这棵松树有 10 英尺,也可能 12 英尺高,可是,对于这个小男孩来说,这棵树已经直插木纹状的春日天空了。首先,父亲把树干周围的旁枝折断。然后,他把一根绳子系在腰间,爬到了树的中段。莱恩仰望着,惊叹父亲灵巧地爬到距离地面这么高的地方。他一下来,就把绳子的另一头递给了儿子。

"要是你还没准备好的时候树就倒了,那可怎么办呢?"

"所以我才要你抓住绳子啊。"他的父亲开玩笑说。"如果树倒的话,把它从我身上扯下来。"莱恩希望他只是开玩笑。一个五岁的孩子要承担避免父亲被压伤的责任,这压力也太大了。

"他不会有事的。"他父亲喊道。莱恩转过身来,看见妈妈从高高的前门廊往下看。"我开始砍树时,你一定要留在我后面。"他父亲告诉他,然后再次回头看了他一眼。

"好的。"莱恩说道,环顾四周,不知道自己应该站多远。当他转过身来时,他的母亲已经走了。然后他问道:"我们为什么要把它砍掉?"

"因为你妈妈想要把它砍掉。"

为了搞笑，莱恩背诵了他最近看过的一部电影中的一句台词："那么，妈妈说什么，你就做什么呗？"

他父亲哈哈大笑。"嗯，她说得对。应该把它砍下来。看看这个。"他指着树上几个不同地方渗出的糖似的液体说道。

"这是什么？"

"树脂。"他父亲说道。

"树脂是什么呀？"莱恩一边问，一边擦去树皮上的黏性液体，然后用手指搓着。

"就像树的血。"

"树为什么会滴血呢？"

"可能有很多原因。"他父亲说道，"滴一点点是正常的，可是如果它长时间一直在流血，就是出问题了：可能是感染了细菌、真菌，也可能是因为昆虫，甚至啄木鸟。你早上有没有听到啄木鸟的声音？"

"有时候能听到。"莱恩一边说，一边擦着工装裤上的树脂。

"它也可能在上一季的飓风中受损。最近发生了很多事情。"莱恩的父亲仰起头来，看着灰蒙蒙的天空说道。"飓风很快就要卷土重来了，我们可不希望树砸进屋里。"

不久前的一天晚上，莱恩和妈妈在客厅里，一辆车在街上轰隆作响。刺耳尖锐的声音很大，持续的时间也很长，他在脑海里能看到汽车从前窗撞了进来。他想到自己家的树也会像这样，好不到哪去。

当莱恩思绪万千的时候，他父亲用手指抹一些树脂，涂在儿子的额头上。

"嘿！"莱恩往后一跳。半是生气，但不知怎么地，还半是欢喜。

"我祝福你，我的儿子。"他的父亲像演戏似的说道。然后他用链锯在树的前面锯开了一个V形缺口。春天的气息被一种莱恩无法描绘的气味掩盖了。他一直等到他父亲把缺口锯得快断以后才问到底是什么味道。"是树的味道，"他父亲说，"它快要死了。"

莱恩几乎听不到他父亲说话，因为他的耳朵还都是电锯的嗡嗡声。他与那棵树没有特别紧密的联系。他在树下面玩了无数次，但现在刚刚承认它的存在，现在它却即将永远地消失了。

"你想帮我拉吗？"

尽管莱恩为这棵树感到难过，但他还是忍不住抓住这个机会。"这就像一场拔河比赛。"

"站在我前面。"他父亲说。那男孩照做了，额头上还留着树脂。树脂弄得他痒了起来，但他不愿意松开手里的绳子去抓挠。"你准备好了吗？"

莱恩点了点头，他们一起拉了起来。他不知道自己实际上能帮多少忙，但他竭尽所能。他的脚后跟陷在土里使劲儿地蹬着。他的背悬在半空中，一直抓着绳子。"就这样。"他父亲喊道。有一个长长的、被拉长的折断声。这和莱恩以前听过的任何声音都不一样。他紧绷着脸——就像他紧张时经常做的那样——看着树干向地面坠落。当地面震动的那一刻，莱恩也跟着一抖。然而，他的父亲仍然坚定不移，没有畏缩。

莱恩又感觉到母亲的目光在盯着他们，但犹豫着没有回头去看。他父亲一定也有同样的感觉。他转过身来，快速点了点头。"他很好。"他告诉莱恩的母亲。她又在门廊上站了一会儿，然后回到屋里。

父亲和儿子走到树前，俯视着站了一会儿。两人都没有说话。真可惜，莱恩想。除了出血点，这棵树大部分枝干看起来很健康。但后来他注意到仍然从地上伸出来的那部分。它不像其他的部分那么新鲜，它腐烂了，从根部剥落了。

"这树几岁了？"莱恩问道。

"我不知道。"他父亲耸了耸肩。"我和你母亲搬进来的时候，它就在这里，可能比你大，我想大概有十五或二十岁，但也可能更大。"

"我想象不到它有这么大。"

他父亲哈哈大笑。"等你到我这个年纪，就能想象到啦。"

"我都等不及到你这么大啦。"

"为什么会这样？"

"只有长到你这么大，我才可以做你现在能做的所有事情——比如爬上那么高的树，足够强壮把树拉倒。可我现在什么都做不了。什么本领也没有。"

他父亲又哈哈大笑起来。"你看到这个了吗？"他指着从地上伸出的腐烂树干问道。

"看到了。"莱恩说道。"这就是树脂滴下来的原因吗？"

"可能是吧。"他父亲说。"不管是什么问题，它从底部开始，一直向上发展。你知道这是怎么回事吗？"

"你以前说过：可能有很多原因。"

"是的，但主要是这棵树变老了。"他父亲说道。"你看，当一个生命还年轻的时候，都会很无力。然而，这并不一定就是坏事。柔弱其实是一件美好的事情，这意味着这些生命容易受到影响，对周围的一切仍有弹性。另一方面，力量使一切生命变得坚硬和不可饶恕。它变得干燥和老化。柔弱是一切，力量是虚空，因为弱者代表了一切刚刚开始，而强者却代表着走向死亡。"

然后他们开始处理这棵树。父亲用链锯锯了一下，莱恩把他能搬得动的所有东西都搬到院子角落里铺着油布的木架上。他来来回回地跑，每次都比上一次更用力；肩上负重，手上的木块又脆又硬。但他不停地来回走着，穿过雾蒙蒙的草坪。他用尽了所有的力气。他渴望将来会拥有的那种力量——那种力量将为树脂最终耗尽的那一天做准备，使我们有备无患。

他父亲给他抹在头上的树脂还在让他痒，但莱恩在抓挠它时确保尽可能地小心。他想尽可能让树脂在那里待得更久些。

Sap

By Anthony Perrotta

Layne stood to the side, watching as his father prepared to cut down the pine tree in their backyard. The tree stood at ten, maybe twelve feet tall, but as far as the boy was concerned, it might as well have reached the grainy, spring sky. First, the father removed whatever branches there were on the sides. Then, he climbed up and tied one end of the rope above the middle of the tree. Layne looked up, amazed at how his father maneuvered himself so far off the ground. Once he made it back down, he handed his son the other end of the rope.

"What if it falls before you're ready?"

"That's why I'm having you hold the rope," his father joked. "If it does, pull it away from me." Layne hoped he was only kidding. The pressure of having to stop his father from being crushed at five-years-old was too great.

"He'll be fine," his father called out. Layne turned around to see his mother peering down at them from the elevated front porch. "When I start cutting, just make sure you stay back," his father told him before shooting another look back up.

"Okay," Layne said, looking around, wondering how far back he should stand. By the time he turned back around, his mother was gone. He then asked, "Why are we cutting it down?"

"Because your mother wants it down."

Trying to be funny, Layne recited a line from some movie that he recently saw: "So, you just do everything Mom tells you?"

His father laughed. "Well, she's right. It needs to come down. Look at this," he said, pointing to the sugary liquid that oozed from several different spots on the tree.

"What's that?"

"Sap," his father said.

"What is it?" Layne asked as he wiped some of the sticky fluid off the hard bark and rubbed it between his fingers.

"It's like the blood of a tree."

"Why is it dripping?"

"It could be a bunch of reasons," his father said. "Some dripping is okay, but when it's been bleeding for as long as this one, something is wrong: bacteria, fungus, insects, even woodpeckers. Do you ever hear the woodpeckers in the morning?"

"Sometimes." Layne said, wiping the sap on his cargo pants.

"It could also have been damaged during one of the hurricanes last season. There's been a lot more lately," Layne's father said, looking up at the gray sky. "The hurricanes will be starting up again soon. We don't want the tree falling into the house."

One night, not too long ago, Layne was in the living room with his mother when a car pealed out in the street. The screech was long and loud, and in his mind, he could see the car crashing through the front window. The thought of their own tree doing just that was no better.

As Layne's mind wandered, his father dabbed his finger with some of the sap and rubbed it across his son's forehead.

"Hey!" Layne jumped backward, half annoyed, but somehow half joyous.

"I bless you, my son," his father dramatized. He then proceeded to cut a V-shaped notch into the front of the tree with his chainsaw. The springtime air was masked by a smell that Layne couldn't quite place. He waited until his father was finished weakening the base before he asked what it was. "It's the tree," his father said. "It's dying."

Layne could barely hear his father speak, as his ears were still ringing from the chainsaw. He didn't have a particularly strong connection to the tree. He played underneath it countless times, but was only now acknowledging its existence; now that it would be gone forever.

"Do you want to help me pull?"

As sorry as he felt for the tree, Layne couldn't help but jump at the chance. "It'll be like a game of tug of war."

"Get in front of me," his father said. The boy did, the sap still on his forehead. It itched, but he wasn't willing to take his hands off the rope to scratch it. "Are you ready?"

Layne nodded, and together, they pulled. He didn't know how much he was actually helping, but Layne pulled with everything he had. His heels, digging into the soil. His back, suspended in mid-air as he kept holding onto the rope. "There it goes," his father hollered. There was a long, drawn-out snap. It was unlike anything Layne had ever heard before. He clenched his face—as he often did when he was nervous—watching as the trunk plummeted towards the earth. Layne shuddered as the ground quaked. His father, however, remained unflinching.

Layne felt his mother's eyes on them again, but was hesitant to look back. His father must have felt the same thing. He turned and gave a quick nod. "He's fine," he told Layne's mother. Again, she stood on the porch for a moment before heading back inside.

The father and son walked over to the tree and stood over it for a moment, looking down. Neither spoke. It was a shame, Layne thought. Other than the bleeding spots, the tree, for the most part, looked healthy. But then he noticed the part that was still sticking up from the ground. It wasn't as fresh as the rest. It was decayed, flaking at the roots.

"How old was the tree?" Layne asked.

"I don't know," his father shrugged. "It was here when your mother and I moved in; before you were born. I would say fifteen or twenty-years-old, but it could be older."

"I can't imagine being that old."

His father laughed. "Just wait until you're my age."

"I can't wait until I'm your age."

"Why is that?"

"So, I can do all the things you do—like climb a tree that high, and be strong enough to pull it down. I can't do anything yet. Nothing."

His father laughed again. "Do you see this?" he asked, pointing to the rotted part of the trunk, sticking up from the ground.

"Yes," Layne said. "Is that why the sap was dripping?"

"Probably," his father said. "Whatever the problem was, it started at the bottom and was working its way up. Do you know how it got this way?"

"You said before: it could be a bunch of things."

"Yes, but mainly, the tree got old," his father said. "You see, when something is young, it's helpless. Now, that's not necessarily a bad thing. It's actually a beautiful thing to be weak. That means something is sensitive, but still resilient to everything around it. Strength, on the other hand, makes everything hard and unforgiving. It becomes dry and jaded. Weakness is everything, and strength is nothing, because weakness is only the beginning, and anything that is strong is already dead."

They then began disposing of the tree. The father cut with the chainsaw while Layne carried whatever pieces he could manage over to the tarp-covered firewood rack in the corner of the yard. Each time he went back and forth was harder than the last; the weight on his shoulders, the crisp, rigid wood on his hands. But he kept going, back and forth, across the misty lawn. It took all the strength that he had. And he longed for the strength that he would have in the future—the strength that prepares us for the day that the sap finally runs out.

The splotch that his father put on his head still itched, but Layne made sure to be as careful as possible while scratching it. He wanted to leave it for as long as he could.